KNOCKEMSTIFF

DONALD RAY POLLOCK

KNOCKEMSTIFF

Donald Ray Pollock grew up in Knockemstiff, Ohio. He dropped out of high school to work in a meatpacking plant and then spent over thirty years employed in a paper mill in southern Ohio. Currently, he is a graduate student in the MFA program at Ohio State University. His stories have appeared in the *Berkeley Fiction Review*, the *Journal*, *Third Coast*, *Chiron Review*, *Sou'wester*, *Boulevard*, and *Folio*, and he has contributed essays on politics to the Op-Ed page of *The New York Times*.

KNOCKEMSTIFF

KNOCKEMSTIFF

DONALD RAY POLLOCK

ANCHOR BOOKS

A Division of Random House, Inc.

New York

FIRST ANCHOR BOOKS EDITION, MARCH 2009

Copyright © 2008 by Donald Ray Pollock

All rights reserved. Published in the United States by Anchor Books,
a division of Random House, Inc., New York, and in Canada by Random
House of Canada Limited, Toronto. Originally published in hardcover in
the United States by Doubleday, a division of Random House, Inc.,
New York, in 2008.

Anchor Books and colophon are registered trademarks
of Random House, Inc.

Some of these stories have appeared in slightly different form in the
following magazines: "Bactine," "Fish Sticks," and "Giganthomachy" in the
Journal; "Discipline" and "Lard" in *Third Coast*; "Honolulu" in
Chiron Review; "Assailants," "Holler," and "Hair's Fate" in *Sou'wester*;
"Real Life" in *Boulevard*; "I Start Over" in the *Berkeley Fiction Review*.

The Library of Congress has cataloged the Doubleday edition as follows:
Pollock, Donald Ray, 1954–
Knockemstiff / Donald Ray Pollock.
p. cm.
1. Knockemstiff (Ohio)—Social life and customs—Fiction. I. Title.
PS3616.O5694K56 2008
813'.6—dc22
2007039806

Anchor ISBN: 978-0-767-92830-4

Book design by Casey Hampton
Map art by David Cain

www.anchorbooks.com

Printed in the United States of America
10 9 8 7 6 5 4 3 2

FOR PATSY

All Americans come from Ohio originally, if only briefly.

—DAWN POWELL

CONTENTS

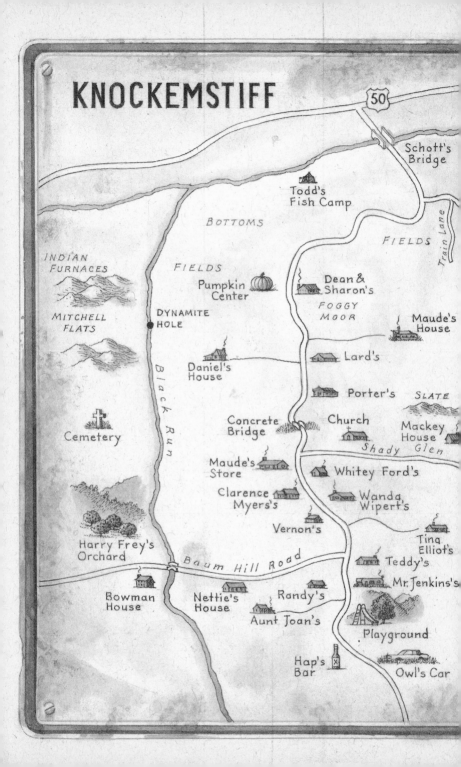

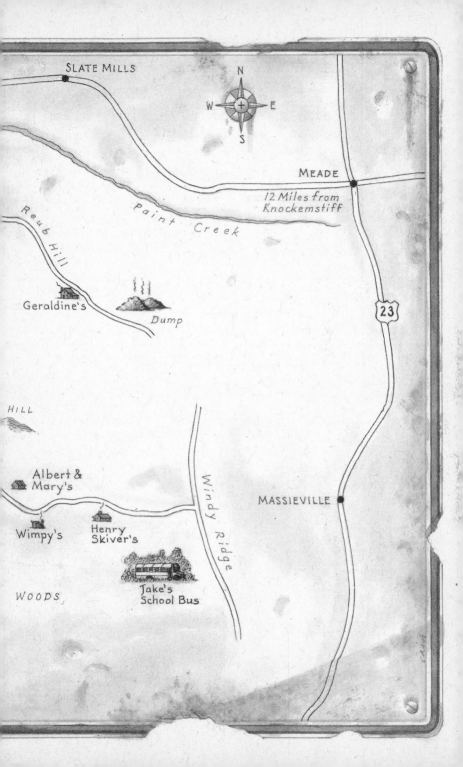

KNOCKEMSTIFF

REAL LIFE

MY FATHER SHOWED ME HOW TO HURT A MAN ONE AUGUST night at the Torch Drive-in when I was seven years old. It was the only thing he was ever any good at. This was years ago, back when the outdoor movie experience was still a big deal in southern Ohio. *Godzilla* was playing, along with some sorry-ass flying saucer movie that showed how pie pans could take over the world.

It was hotter than a fat lady's box that evening, and by the time the cartoon began playing on the big plywood screen, the old man was miserable. He kept bitching about the heat, sopping the sweat off his head with a brown paper bag. Ross County hadn't had any rain in two months. Every morning my mother turned the kitchen radio to KB98 and listened to Miss Sally Flowers pray for a thunderstorm. Then she'd go outside and stare at the empty white sky that hung over the holler like a sheet. Sometimes I still think about her standing in that brittle brown grass, stretching her neck in hopes of seeing just one lousy dark cloud.

"Hey, Vernon, watch this," she said that night. Ever since we'd parked, she'd been trying to show the old man that she could stick a hot dog down her throat without messing up her shiny lipstick. You've got to understand, my mother hadn't been out of Knockemstiff all summer. Just seeing a couple of red lights had made her all goosey. But every time she gagged on that wiener, the ropy muscles in the back of my old man's neck twisted a little tighter, made it seem as if his head was going to pop off any second. My older sister, Jeanette, had used her head and played sick all day, then talked them into letting her stay at a neighbor's house. So there I was, stuck in the backseat by myself, chewing the skin off my fingers, and hoping Mom wouldn't piss him off too much before Godzilla stomped the guts out of Tokyo.

But really, it was already too late. Mom had forgotten to pack the old man's special cup, and so everything was shot in the ass as far as he was concerned. He couldn't even muster a chuckle for Popeye, let alone get excited about his wife doing tricks with a wrinkled-up Oscar Mayer. Besides, my old man hated movies. "Screw a bunch of make-believe," he'd say whenever someone mentioned seeing the latest John Wayne or Robert Mitchum. "What the hell's wrong with real life?" He'd only agreed to the drive-in in the first place because of all the hell Mom had raised about his new car, a 1965 Impala he'd brought home the night before.

It was the third set of wheels in a year. We lived on soup beans and fried bread, but drove around Knockemstiff like rich people. Just that morning, I'd heard my mother get on the phone and rag to her sister, the one who lived in town. "The sonofabitch is crazy, Margie," she said. "We couldn't even pay the electric bill last month." I was sitting in front of the dead TV, watching watery blood trickle down her pale calves. She'd tried to shave them with the old man's straight razor, but her legs were like sticks of butter. A black fly kept buzzing around her bony ankles, dodging her mad slaps. "I mean it, Margie," she said into the black mouthpiece, "I'd be outta this hellhole in a minute if it wasn't for these kids."

As soon as *Godzilla* started, the old man pulled the ashtray out of the dash and poured a drink in it from his bottle. "Good Lord, Vernon," my mom said. She was holding the hot dog in midair, getting ready to have another go at it.

"Hey, I told you, I ain't drinkin' from no bottle. You start that shit, you end up a goddamn wino." He took a slug from the ashtray, then gagged and spit a soggy cigarette butt out the window. He'd been at it since noon, showing off the new ride to his good-time buddies. There was already a dent in one of the side panels.

After a couple more sips from the ashtray, the old man jerked the door open and swung his skinny legs out. Puke sprayed from his mouth, soaking the cuffs of his blue work pants with Old Grand-Dad. The station wagon next to us started up and moved to another spot down the row. He hung his head between his legs for a minute or two, then rose up and wiped his chin with the back of his hand. "Bobby," he said to me, "one more of your mama's greasy taters and they'll be plantin' your old daddy." My old man didn't eat enough to keep a rat alive, but anytime he threw up his whiskey, he blamed it on Mom's cooking.

Mom gave up, wrapped the hot dog in a napkin, and handed it back to me. "Remember, Vernon," she warned, "you gotta drive us home."

"Shoot," he said, lighting a cigarette, "this car drives its own self." Then he tipped up the ashtray and finished off the rest of his drink. For a few minutes, he stared at the screen and sank slowly into the padded upholstery like a setting sun. My mom reached over and turned the speaker that was hanging in the window down a notch. Our only hope was that the old man would pass out before the entire night was ruined. But as soon as Raymond Burr landed at the Tokyo airport, he shot straight up in his seat, then turned and glared back at me with his bloodshot eyes. "Goddamn it, boy," he said, "how many times I gotta tell you about bitin' them fingernails? You sound like a mouse chewin' through a fuckin' sack of corn."

"Leave him be, Vernon," my mother said. "That ain't what he does anyway."

"Jesus, what's the difference?" he said, scratching the whiskers on his neck. "Hard to tell where he's had those dick skinners."

I pulled my fingers out of my mouth and sat on my hands. It was the only way I could keep away from them whenever the old man was around. That whole summer, he'd been threatening to coat me clear to the elbows with chicken shit to break me of the habit. He splashed more whiskey in his ashtray, and gulped it down with a shudder. Just as I began edging slowly across the seat to sit behind my mother, the dome light popped on. "C'mon, Bobby," he said, "we gotta take a leak."

"But the show just started, Vernon," Mom protested. "He's been waiting all summer to see this."

"Hey, you know how he is," the old man said, loud enough for the people in the next row to hear. "He sees that Godzilla thing, I don't want him pissin' all over my new seats." Sliding out of the car, he leaned against the metal speaker post and stuffed his T-shirt into his baggy pants.

I got out reluctantly and followed my old man as he weaved across the gravel lot. Some teenage girls in culottes strutted by us, their legs illuminated by the movie screen's glimmering light. When he stopped to stare at them, I crashed into the back of his legs and fell down at his feet. "Jesus Christ, boy," he said, jerking me up by the arm like a rag doll, "you gotta get your head out of your ass. You act more like your damn mother every day."

The cinder-block building in the middle of the drive-in lot was swarming with people. The loud rattling projector was up front, the concession stand in the middle, and the johns in the back. The smell of piss and popcorn hung in the hot dead air like insecticide. In the restroom, a row of men and boys leaned over a long green metal trough with their dicks hanging out. They all stared straight ahead at a wall painted the color of mud. Others were lined up behind them on the wet sticky floor, rocking on the toes of their shoes, impatiently waiting their turn. A fat man in bib overalls and a ragged straw hat tottered out of a wooden stall munching on a Zero candy bar and the old man shoved me inside, slamming the door behind me.

I flushed the commode and stood there holding my breath, pretending to take a leak. Bits and pieces of movie dialogue drifted in from outside and I was trying to imagine the parts I was missing when the old man started banging on the flimsy door. "Damn, boy, what's taking you so long?" he yelled. "You beatin' your meat in there?" He pounded again, and I heard someone laugh. Then he said, "I tell you what, these fuckin' kids will drive you crazy."

I zipped up and stepped out of the stall. The old man was handing a cigarette to a porky guy with sawdust combed through his greasy black hair. A purple stain shaped like a wedge of pie covered the belly of his dirty shirt. "I shit you not, Cappy," my father was telling the man, "this boy's scared of his own goddamn shadow. A fuckin' bug's got more balls."

"Yeah, I know what you mean," Cappy said. He bit the filter off the cigarette and spat it on the concrete floor. "My sister's got one like that. Poor little guy, he can't even bait a hook."

"Bobby shoulda been a girl," the old man said. "Goddamn it, when I was that age, I was choppin' wood for the stove."

Cappy lit the cigarette with a long wooden match he pulled from his shirt pocket and said with a shrug, "Well, things was different back then, Vern." Then he stuck the match in his ear and twirled it around inside his head.

"I know, I know," the old man went on, "but it still makes you wonder what the fuck's gonna happen to this goddamn country someday."

Suddenly a man wearing black-framed glasses stepped from his place in line at the urinal and tapped my old man on the shoulder. He was the biggest sonofabitch I'd ever seen; his fat head nearly touched the ceiling. His arms were the size of fence posts. A boy my size stood behind him, wearing a pair of brightly colored swimming trunks and a T-shirt that had a faded picture of Davy Crockett on the front of it. He had a fresh waxy crew cut and orange pop stains on his chin. Every time he took a breath, a Bazooka bubble bloomed from his mouth like a round pink flower. He looked happy, and I hated him instantly.

"Watch your language," the man said. His loud voice boomed across the room and everyone turned to look at us.

The old man whirled around and rammed his nose into the big man's chest. He bounced back and looked up at the giant towering over him. "Goddamn," he said.

The big man's sweaty face began to turn red. "Didn't you understand me?" he said to my father. "I asked you to watch your cussing. I don't want my son hearing that kind of talk."

Then he said slowly, like he was dealing with a retard, "I . . . won't . . . ask . . . you . . . again."

"You didn't ask me the first fuckin' time," my old man shot back. He was tough as bark but rail thin back in those days, and he never knew when to keep his mouth shut. He looked around at the crowd starting to gather, then turned to Cappy and winked.

"Oh, you think it's funny?" the man said. His hands tightened into fists the size of softballs and he made a move toward my father. Someone in the back said, "Kick his ass."

My father took two steps back, dropped his cigarette, and held up his palms. "Now hold on there, buddy. Jesus, I don't mean nothing." Then he lowered his eyes, stood staring at the big man's shiny black shoes for a few seconds. I could see him gnawing on the inside of his mouth. His hands kept opening and closing like the pincers on a crawdad. "Hey," he finally said, "we don't need no trouble here tonight."

The big man glanced at the people watching him. They were all waiting for his next move. His glasses started to slide down his broad nose and he pushed them back up. Taking a deep breath, he swallowed hard, then jabbed a fat finger in my father's bony chest. "Look, I mean what I say," he said, spit flying out of his mouth. "This here is a family place. I don't care if you are a damn drunk. You understand?" I sneaked a look over at the man's son and he stuck his tongue out at me.

"Yeah, I understand all right," I heard my father say quietly.

A smug look came over the big bastard's face. His chest puffed out like a tom turkey's, straining the brown buttons on his clean white shirt. Looking around at the pack of men who were hoping to see a fight, he sighed deeply and shrugged his wide shoulders. "I guess that's it, boys," he said to no one in particular. Then, his hand now resting gently on top of his son's head, he started to turn.

I watched nervously as the disappointed crowd shook their heads and began moving away. I remember wishing I could slide out the door with them. I figured the old man would blame me for the way that things had turned out. But just as Godzilla's screechy, door-hinge roar echoed through the restroom, he leaped forward and drove his fist against the temple of the big man's head. People never believe me, but I once saw him knock a horse out with that same hand. A sickening crack reverberated through the concrete room. The man staggered sideways and all of the air suddenly whooshed out of his body like a fart. His hands waved frantically in the air as if he were grabbing for a lifeline, and then he dropped to the floor with a thud.

The room went quiet for a second, but when the man's son began screaming, my father exploded. He circled around the man, kicking the ribs with his work boots, stomping the left hand until the gold wedding ring cut through to the bone of his finger. Dropping to his knees, he grabbed the man's glasses and snapped them in two, beat him in the face until a tooth popped through one meaty cheek. Then Cappy and three other men grabbed my father from behind and pulled him away. His fists glistened with blood. A thin string of white froth hung from his chin. I heard someone yell to call the cops. Still holding on to my father, Cappy said, "Jesus, Vern, that man's hurt bad."

Just as I looked up from the body lying on the floor into my father's wild eyes, the man's son turned and drilled me in the ear. I covered up my head with my arms and hunkered down as the boy started to flail away at me. "Goddamn you!" I heard my father yell in a hoarse voice. "You back down, I'll blister your ass!" The hot dogs I'd eaten started to come up, and I swallowed them again. I didn't want to fight, but the boy was nothing compared to the old man. I rose up to face him just as he smacked me in the mouth. I drew back and swung wildly. Somehow I managed to strike him in the face. I heard my father yell again and I kept swinging. After three or four punches, the boy dropped his hands and began blubbering, choking on his bubble gum. I looked over at the old man, and he screamed, "Fuck him up!" I hit the boy again and bright red blood sprayed out of his nose.

Breaking loose from the men holding him, my father grabbed me by the arm and pulled me out the doorway. He ran across the parking lot, dragging me along, searching for our car in the dark. Suddenly he stopped and knelt down in front of me. He was gasping for air. "You did good, Bobby," he said, wiping the sweat from his eyes. He gripped me by the shoulders and squeezed. "You did real good."

When we found the car, my father shoved me in the back-seat and lifted the speaker off the window. He let it drop to the ground with a bang and jumped in and started the engine. My mother jerked awake. "Is it over?" she asked sleepily. A crackly voice came over the speaker system pleading for any doctors or nurses to report to the concession stand immediately. "Lord, what happened?" Mom said, straightening up in the seat, rubbing her face.

"Some fat sonofabitch tried to tell us how to talk, that's what," the old man said. "But we showed their asses, didn't we, Bobby?" He gunned the motor. We all looked up at the screen just as Godzilla bit into a high-voltage tower. "Holy shit, boy, that thing's got teeth this long," my old man laughed, spreading his arms wide. Then he leaned over and told my mother in a low voice, "They'll call the law on this one." He reached down and dropped the Chevy into gear.

Punching the accelerator, the old man shot off the little mound we were parked on and fishtailed down the aisle. Loose gravel splattered against the other cars. An old man and woman tripped over each other trying to get out of our way. Horns began blowing, headlights popped on. We tore out of the exit and skidded onto the highway, heading west toward home. An ambulance sped by us, its siren blaring. I looked back at the theater just as the movie screen flickered and went black.

"Agnes, you should have seen him," my old man said, pounding the steering wheel with his bloody hand. "He busted that goddamn brat a good one." He grabbed his bottle from under the seat, uncapped it, and took a long slug. "This is the best night of my fucking life!" he yelled out the window.

"You got Bobby in a fight?"

"Damn straight, I did," the old man said.

My mother leaned over the front seat and felt my head with her hands, peered at my face in the dark. "Bobby, are you hurt?" she asked me.

"I got blood on me," I said.

"My God, Vernon," she said. "What have you done now, you sick bastard?"

I looked up just as he bashed my mother with his forearm. Her head bounced against the window. "You sonofabitch!" she cried, covering her face with her hands.

"Don't baby him," the old man said. "And don't call me no bastard neither."

I scooted across the seat and sat behind my father as we

raced home. Every time he passed a car, he took another pull from the bottle. Wind rushed through his open window and dried my sweat. The Impala felt like it was floating above the highway. *You did good*, I kept saying to myself, over and over. It was the only goddamn thing my old man ever said to me that I didn't try to forget.

L ATER THE SOUND OF AN APPROACHING STORM WOKE ME up. I was lying in my bed, still in my clothes. Through my window, I saw lightning flash over the Mitchell Flats. A rumbling wall of thunder rolled across the holler, followed closely by a high, horrible wail; and I thought of Godzilla and the movie that I'd missed. It was only after the thunder faded into the distance that I realized that the wail was just the sound of my old man getting sick in the bathroom.

My bedroom door opened and my mother walked in holding a lighted candle. "Bobby?" she said. I pretended to be asleep. She leaned over me, brushed my sore cheek with her soft hand. Then she reached up and closed my window. In the candlelight, I sneaked a look at the bruise spreading across her face like a smear of grape jelly.

She tiptoed out of the room, leaving the door ajar, and walked down the hall. "There," I heard her say to my father, "is that better?"

"I think I fucked it up," my father said. "That bastard's head was hard as a rock."

"You shouldn't drink, Vernon," my mom said.

"Is he asleep?"

"He's wore out."

"I'd bet a paycheck he broke that kid's nose, the way the blood came out," my father said.

"We better go to bed," my mom said.

"I couldn't believe it, Agnes. That fucking kid was twice Bobby's size, I swear to God."

"He's just a boy, Vernon."

They walked slowly past my door, leaning into each other, and went into their bedroom. I heard my mother say, "No way," but then after a few minutes, their bed began to squeak like a rusty seesaw. Outside, the storm finally cut loose, and big drops of rain began pounding the tin roof of the house. I heard my mother moan, my father call out for Jesus. A bolt of lightning arced across the black sky, and long shadows moved about on the bare plaster walls of my room. I pulled the thin sheet over my head and stuck my fingers in my mouth. A sweet, salty taste stung my busted lip, ran over my tongue. It was the other boy's blood, still on my hands.

As my parents' bed thumped loudly against the floor in the next room, I lapped the blood off my knuckles. The dried flakes dissolved in my mouth, turning my spit to syrup. Even after I'd swallowed all the blood, I kept licking my hands. I tore at the skin with my teeth. I wanted more. I would always want more.

DYNAMITE HOLE

I WAS COMING DOWN OFF THE MITCHELL FLATS WITH THREE arrowheads in my pocket and a dead copperhead hung around my neck like an old woman's scarf when I caught a boy named Truman Mackey fucking his own little sister in the Dynamite Hole. I'd been hunting flints all morning up around the old Indian furnaces and was headed for the store down in Knockemstiff to trade them for some potted meat and crackers. Maude Speakman allowed me forty cents for each one I brought her, and then she sold them over again to some man from Meade who delivered her gas every Tuesday.

It was hot that day, and as I crossed Black Run, knee deep in the water and fighting the green flies that were swarming around the snake's mashed-up head, I heard some splashing around the bend. I stopped and listened close for a minute, then cut back over and sneaked up to the edge of the big hole that a county road crew had blasted in the creek years ago digging for gravel. I hoped to see something is all, thought maybe I'd have some fun with that dead snake if it turned out to be that goddamn gang of boys who'd been throwing rocks at my old school bus, the one Henry Skiver let me stay in up behind his property. Henry's daddy used to keep the bus for a chicken house, but I shoveled it out good, and it wasn't so bad after that. Lately, though, those boys had busted so many holes in the top of it that every time it rained I might as well been living in a bathtub.

I damn near swallowed my cud when I got up there and saw the Mackey boy had his sister down on her hands and knees at the edge of the water and him behind her with no clothes on. I stepped back off the path a ways, then eased down on the ground and crawled up behind some chokecherry bushes to watch. My heart started beating so big I thought it was going to pop out of my chest, and I was afraid they'd hear all the noise it was making, but Truman and her just went on about their business like they were the only two people on this little patch of God's wicked earth.

NOWADAYS I RECKON MOST PEOPLE WOULD STARVE TO death if they tried to live like me, but I learned years ago that a man can get by in this world without being somebody's nigger if he don't mind what he eats for supper. Back when I was nineteen, they started drafting boys for the big war against the Germans, and I hid on top of the Mitchell Flats for almost three years with nothing but a penknife and a ball of twine I stole from Floyd Bowman's barn. My old man threw a fit when I told him I wasn't going to answer the call, spit all kinds of names in my face like I wasn't nothing but dirt. "Jake, you goddamn chickenshit, I won't be able to face people around here you run away," he told me, but I left that night anyway. I'd never been more than two miles away from Knockemstiff, Ohio, in my whole life. And though there have been plenty of days I still regret I didn't try to make him see things my way that night, I guess taking off just seemed easier at the time. Hell, how could I have told that old man, the way they were drafting and killing boys left and right, that I wasn't afraid of the fighting nearly as much as I was scared of leaving the holler?

THAT MACKEY GIRL COULDN'T HAVE BEEN MORE THAN twelve or so, but she was backing up against her brother like she'd been at it for quite a while. Truman was maybe fifteen or sixteen years old, and long and skinny as a horseweed, same as his mouthy old man. He'd push it in her a few times and get her all squirmy, and then they'd both jump up and raise their arms into the sticky air and yell, "Jesus, save me!" And every time they said it, they'd fall backward in the hole laughing, and then Truman would get up behind her again, that filthy brown water running off him onto her, and they'd do it all over. And Lord, though my family never was one for religion, the first time I heard those words coming out of their mouths like that, they cut me near as bad as the ones my old man called me the night I left his house for good. I started to get up and come out from behind the bushes, figuring if I let them know I was around, they'd run on home and maybe think twice about what they'd been doing. But then I didn't, and the longer I laid there and watched them, the more I talked myself into believing that they'd just found their own little way of praying, and that maybe they really did want the Savior or even somebody else to come down and wipe away their sins.

WHEN I TOOK OFF THAT TIME TO GO HIDE UP ON THE flats from the military, the old man wouldn't allow me to take nothing but the bibs I was wearing and my old mackinaw and that penknife. I went awful hungry those three years, and I got used to that empty feeling eating away at my insides, which I know ain't nearly as bad as some of the feelings people carry around with them. I mostly lived on field corn and what squirrels and rabbits I could knock in the head and the sunfish and crawdads I scooped up out of Black Run. In the winter, I stayed in a tepee I made out of corn shocks, and in the good weather I slept underneath a briar patch or else back in this hollow log that laid up behind Harry Frey's orchard. Once in a while, I'd slip down to the holler in the middle of the night and go to my family's house. My mother would keep a watch out for me and leave me some biscuits in a poke behind the smokehouse and maybe a piece of meat if there was any. Looking back on it, I guess I can recall only one time in my life when I knew what it was like to have a full belly, and that was just a few years ago when Maude gave me a big roll of old-fashioned bologna she thought was going bad. She said maybe I could feed it to the stray beagle dog that was following me around at the time, but I bought a loaf of bread and took it back to the school bus and ate the whole damn thing myself before I got sick. It must have took a month for me to get over that, and I ain't never been able to eat more than just a little bit since.

I CREPT UP CLOSER TO THE BANK, AND PRETTY SOON I WAS near enough that the water splashed on me whenever those kids did their little dance. It was a beautiful sight, the way the sunlight floated down through the sycamore trees on that young girl and turned everything she did into something sweet and golden. I felt myself growing hard against the ground through my old bibs, and I guess watching her push back and forth on her brother made me all light-headed. I remember holding that dead copperhead up to my lips and kissing it the same way I'd seen men kiss their women in their bedrooms at night. Maybe it was the heat, or maybe it was because of the things I was seeing, but all of a sudden it seemed as if everything inside me started swirling around like a storm cloud.

I'D BEEN HIDING UP ON THE FLATS FOR ABOUT A YEAR WHEN I came down to the holler one night hoping to get some biscuits and my family was gone. The old house was empty, and somebody had pulled all the windows out and took the doors right off the hinges. They'd left a letter in the smokehouse that said my little brother Bill had been killed on some island out in the ocean and that they'd gone back to Kentucky, which is where my old man was from before. I didn't even know my brother was in the army until I read that letter, and he couldn't have been much older than Truman Mackey when he got himself killed. I stood there looking at my sister's handwriting and wishing they'd taken me with them, but the old man had always favored Bill over the rest of us, and I guess it made him sad that he lost the youngest instead of me. I never saw them again, and after that, I never could get rid of that feeling that I wasn't much welcome nowhere in the world.

It was late that same summer when the military finally sent two boys in green uniforms out to hunt for me, and I've always wondered if my old man didn't tell them where to look. You could hear them boys tromping through the woods from a mile away; and when I saw there were only two of them, I came out and let them see me. I led them on a damn goose chase up and down the hills all the rest of that day, just keeping ahead of them enough they couldn't get a shot at me. By evening, I could tell they was all wore out, and I heard them cussing the hillbillies and the briars, and the fatter one was telling the other about panthers coming out at night and that they better get down off the hill before dark. But I wasn't ready for them to leave yet, so I snapped a branch off a tree right behind them, and they jumped up and started the chase all over again. And that's when I led them down into that little holler I'd been fixing up in case I ever had any trouble.

SOMEHOW, I ENDED UP WITH THAT LITTLE MACKEY GIRL IN my arms. I don't expect no one would ever believe me, but it was like the dark cloud busted in the top of my skull, and I opened my eyes and there was an angel. I ran my hands through her wet hair and tried to settle her down, but she kept blubbering and going on about her brother. I looked over and saw Truman all bloody about the head, his pecker still hard and sticking up out of the water like a piece of carved wood. Then the girl saw the snake I had wrapped around my neck and she started screaming so loud I was afraid they'd hear her clear down on the road. So I held the snake's head up to her face and told her I'd turn it loose on her if she couldn't be quiet. But that made her carry on all that much more, and finally I had to get my hands around her neck and squeeze a little bit, just enough to settle her down until I could get straight on what had happened to that boy. Her face turned red as a raspberry, and her eyes flipped back in her head until only the whites were showing, and I let up on her and pushed her nose down in the gravel. I remember a mud dauber landed close to her ear, and I smashed it against the side of her head with my hand. She got easy after that, and I got my bibs down and slipped inside her the way I'd seen her brother do. I tried to get her to say some things like I'd heard a couple of those women do with their men, but this one, all she wanted to do was whimper and cry.

THE PLACE I LED THOSE MILITARY TO THAT EVENING wasn't nothing but a little washed-out gully with slate rock and dead timber lying in the bottom of it, and I'd been catching copperheads and throwing them in there all summer. By the time those two boys got to the spot I'd picked out, I'd already climbed up the other side and was looking down on them. Like I said, there was just a little light left, and they were standing down at the lower end of that gully and looking up into it, trying to decide what to do next. I saw one of them light up a smoke, and I was close enough to smell it was store-bought. Then I tossed a rock up ahead of them, and the skinny one said, "By God, Jesse, I think we got that sonofabitch now." They climbed over the dead logs I'd blocked up the lower end with and rushed in, and I saw a big fat bastard pop out of the side of the hill and strike the one boy smack in the face so hard it knocked him backward. He was still trying to pull that snake off his cheek when the other one turned and ran off firing his gun every which way.

I'D NEVER BEEN INSIDE A REAL PERSON BEFORE, AND WHEN I started to finish, it was like everything I'd ever known didn't matter no more. All the hard years and the loneliness flowed out of me and bubbled up inside that little girl like a wet spring coming out of the side of a hill. I still had the snake around me, and I held it up and shook it at the sun and cried out, "Jesus, save me!" because I thought she might like that. But when I pulled loose from her, she started fighting to get away again, and I looked over at the boy and saw the club that had killed him floating by his head. His eyes were wide open and staring up at the puffy clouds stuck in the sky, and the blood coming out of his mouth was turning the water the color of wine. And I realized that no matter what I did, I couldn't stop this thing now. It was already turning some kind of wheel all its own, like the time those boys followed me into that nest of copperheads. I held the girl down with one hand while I tried to reach over for the club. But she was slippery as an eel, and I got afraid that if she got loose, I couldn't run her down. So I clenched both hands around her neck, and this time I didn't let up until there wasn't anything left but her sweet face all bloomed out like a purple flower and a skinny little body turned to wax.

AFTER THAT OTHER MILITARY BOY GOT AWAY THAT NIGHT, I sat up there on top of the knob listening to his buddy moan and cry. Every once in a while, I'd toss a rock down in there beside him, and I'd hear one of the snakes hit him again. He went out of his head about midnight, and I listened to him talk to his mother for a while. He told her some things he shouldn't have told her, but finally, everything went quiet, and I knew he'd give up the ghost. The next morning, the one who ran off came back with some men in a big camouflaged truck, and they must have emptied forty rounds of buckshot into the side of that holler before they'd go in and get that boy's body out. They left me alone after that, and it wasn't until the war was over that they came back, and this time I let them catch me because I was sick and tired of worrying about it all the time. I figured they'd hang me or something, but all they did was stick me in a hospital with some veterans who were shell-shocked and crazy from what they'd seen in the war. There were men in there that couldn't leave their dicks alone and others who'd get down and lick the floor until their tongues were raw and bloody. I spent two years in there, and then one day they just up and turned me loose, paid young Henry Skiver twenty dollars to come get me and take me back to the holler.

I FINALLY LET GO OF THE GIRL AND CLIMBED UP ON THE bank. I know it sounds funny, but once I got my air back, all I could think about was trying to remember that little girl's name. She was right there in front of me, facedown and turning white as snow in that muddy water; and I wanted more than anything to say her name out loud to the sycamore trees. But even though I'd heard her mother holler it plenty of times down where they lived, calling her to supper or to bed, I couldn't recollect it now, and before I could stop myself, I began to weep. I cried like that for a long spell, the first time I guess I ever cried in my life, and I was still crying when I got up and carried her through the water to the other side of the Dynamite Hole.

There was a cave on the far bank that I knew about where the dirt had give way, and I used to reach up inside when I was hunting for turkles. I dunked the little girl under the water like I was baptizing her and kept stuffing her up inside the hole until she got caught. Then I went back across and got the boy and hid him up under the water with his little sister, her in the back and him in the front. There was a pile of dead brush in the water along the deep end and I managed to shove most of it in front of the little cave. When I got done, I gathered up their clothes that they'd hung in some bushes and hid them inside my bibs, and took the club and slung it off into the woods. Then I picked up my copperhead and walked up through the field and down the road.

I went right past the Mackey house on my way up the holler, saw the mother hoeing weeds in her garden patch. The first thing I did was pour some kerosene on those clothes and burn them behind the school bus. Then I skinned the copperhead and hung the skin up to dry, and by the time I got done, I was wore clear out. I crawled inside the bus and pulled off my bibs and fell asleep on my tick. When I woke up, I watched the sun go down behind the flats, and I decided the best thing to do was try to make a belt for myself out of that snakeskin. Then I cut open a can of beans I had hid away, and I'd just started eating them when I heard that Mackey woman down over the hill start yelling for her kids to come home.

EVEN BACK IN THIS HOLLER, A LOT OF THINGS HAVE changed since then. Henry Skiver passed away a couple year ago, but his old woman, Pet, she still allows me to live in the school bus so long as I stay away from her house. There's people from town that's started building fine homes up on the flats now, and I never would have thought I'd see the day when city people would run the copperheads out. And the government must have forgot all about that boy that got himself killed hunting for me because now they send a welfare man clear out from Meade every month just to make sure I'm doing okay. He brings me a bag of groceries and a little envelope of food stamps, and I haven't been what you'd call hungry in a long time.

That Mackey family, they up and left the holler a year or so after their children turned up missing, and I never did hear the straight on where they went off to. I still walk by their house every day I'm able, and it's all boarded up and empty just like mine was that night I came down off the flats looking for some of my mother's biscuits. People still mention those two kids once in a while, but I don't think anybody really gives a damn except for me. Sometimes, when I'm sitting in front of Maude's store and watching the cars go by and I'm dipping my finger into a can of something and smoothing it across some crackers, I can't help but think about them down there in the Dynamite Hole. I like to picture in my head that that's where they play now, hiding under the water behind those dead rotten branches, where the leeches hang, black and shiny as jewels, beating their tiny hearts. And all the time I'm thinking it, I'm saying to myself, "Jesus, save me."

KNOCKEMSTIFF

TINA ELLIOT IS LEAVING TOMORROW, HEADING OFF WITH Boo Nesser to shack up in a trailer next to a Texas oil field, and I feel as bad as the time my mother died. After I close up for the day, I sit out back by the little camper I live in behind Maude Speakman's store, and I drink too many Blue Ribbons. I lean over in my chair and puke up some froth. My throat burns as I light another cigarette and watch a swarm of black gnats gather around the mess. I hear Clarence Myers a couple of houses down raising hell with his old lady about a lost corn knife, and I wonder just how much a person can take. He's bitched about that machete all summer long, and I hope if Juney ever finds it, she sticks it clear through his stupid, toothless head. A carload of boys from the holler keeps racing up and down the road in a '56 Chevy coated with primer, and I can tell by the way they're burning rubber that there will be another wreck somewhere tonight.

Though she's rotten to the core, I reckon I've always loved Tina Elliot, from the first time I laid eyes on her. She came in the store with her mother right after I started working there, just a little-bitty thing, said she'd give me a kiss for a Reese's Peanut Butter Cup. But that was back before she was old enough to do other things, and ever since she started putting out for the boys, she's been looking for someone to take her away. I wish I could have been the one, I really do, but I don't figure I'll ever leave the holler, not even for Tina. I've lived here all my life, like a toadstool stuck to a rotten log, never even wanting to go into town if I can keep from it.

Not too long ago, she told me that I reminded her of a cousin she's got down in Pike County, an old crazy boy who plays with a plastic coin purse all day, talks off-the-wall shit to the birds. I knew she was high on some of the stuff that Boo's always taking, but it hurt me when she said that, made me think about the time my old man took me rabbit hunting. I can still remember the disappointment in his cold, red face because I couldn't pull the trigger that day in the snow. "You done ruined him," he said to my mother when we got back to the house. He must have told the poor woman that a thousand times before he died. Sometimes it scares me to think I will probably spend the rest of my days wishing I'd blown a rabbit's guts clear across Harry Frey's orchard when I was six years old.

The mosquitoes finally drive me inside the camper around midnight, and I watch a Charlie Chan movie on *Armchair Theater*. It always gives me a comfort, watching the TV late at night, thinking about all the other people around Ohio watching the same old movie, maybe even thinking the same old thoughts. I picture them curled up on their couches in their living rooms, and all the lonely little sounds of the night drifting in through their window screens. Maybe it's because Tina is taking off tomorrow, but I get choked up tonight when the movie flickers to an end and the Columbus station signs off the air. I finish my last beer while they play "America the Beautiful" and the big flag whips around in the breeze. Then I crawl into my bunk that's bolted to the wall and lie there listening to those goddamn boys run the dogshit out of that old junker some more.

The sun is coming up over Bishop Hill when I wake up with a sick headache from all the Blue Ribbon. It's the kind of fucking headache that almost makes me wish I'd taken my mother's advice and knocked up a Christian girl who'd lay down the law. It's hot in the camper, and I look outside and see the Pepsi thermometer I got nailed to the outhouse already shows seventy-seven degrees. I pull on a pair of dirty jeans and a clean T-shirt and pump some water from the well into an old dented dishpan. After I wash up, I fill the mop bucket I keep behind the counter. Some of the customers like to see me dip my hands in it before I slice their meat.

I jiggle the lock on the back door and carry the bucket inside the cinder-block building. A log truck rattles down the bumpy road out front, and I think how lucky I am not to be stuck working in the woods in this heat. After I turn on the lights and the gas pumps, I unlock the front door and flip the cardboard sign over that says we're open. The box fan that sits behind the wooden candy case makes a hell of a racket when I start it up, but I leave it on anyway. It blows some dust around, some cigarette ashes, a couple of dead flies dried up in their husks. Maude keeps promising me a new one, but I know she won't come through until the old one locks up completely. She's tight as the bark on a tree when it comes to stuff like that. I pull out the gray metal box we keep under the counter behind a stack of old *True Confessions*, and I start counting money.

I arrange a hundred dollars in small bills and change in the cash register, then pop a couple of aspirins and hunt up a heel of bologna in the meat case from the roll I was cutting on yesterday. I find a bottle of RC Cola slushy with ice in the back of the pop cooler, rip open a bag of green onion potato chips. This is my breakfast, and has been every morning but Sundays for the past twelve years. As I stick my hand down in the chip bag, I think that even if I was to go away with Tina, I'd probably still keep eating the same thing. Then I catch myself and try to laugh it off. It's crazy to think that kind of shit, I know, but I been doing it so long now, I have a hard time stopping myself. The old man used to say I lived in a dream world. I peel the skin off the bologna heel with my thumb, pitch it in the trash. Maybe I'll stop wishing for things I can't have once Tina's gone for good.

I've been working in the store since I was sixteen years old and now I'm twenty-eight. Maude hired me right after my old man got his legs cut off up in Michigan. He was working around Flat Rock with a section gang on the DT&I Railroad, and he slipped in the snow and went under a railcar loaded with ties they were shoving off on a siding. Though he hated being away from the holler, the railroad was the best paying job he'd ever had. Every time he came home for the weekend, he joked, "It's so goddamn flat up there I can't stand up straight." The old man didn't last long after the accident, and the day we laid his box in the frozen ground, I quit school to help my mother hang on to the little house he'd bought us. We kept things afloat for a while, but then she got her cancer and the bank took the house back anyway. That was when Maude bought the camper and set it up behind the store for me to live in. It's shaped like a lunch box on wheels. Sometimes I can't help thinking it's the same size as a prison cell.

I finish my breakfast and break open a fresh pack of Camels. Maude pays me thirty dollars a week, allows me one pack of smokes a day and whatever I can scrounge to eat out of the store. I open up at seven in the morning and work until whatever time she decides to show her face in the evening. It's not a hard life, not like my old man's was, but some days it's a long one, especially if Maude don't come in at all. I keep a few Blue Ribbons stashed in the bottom of the meat case for times like that. She gives me Sundays off because selling cigarettes and candy on the Sabbath isn't good business around here. Even old Maude tries to put on a good act when it comes down to the Lord's day. The Shady Glen Church of Christ in Christian Union sits only a couple hundred yards away from the store, and I wake up every Sunday morning to the crying and clamoring of people who fear God.

By midmorning, I've waited on twenty or so customers: loggers needing chain-saw oil and gasoline, old men after Doan's Liver Pills and honey loaf, little kids trading pop bottles for SweeTarts and cigarettes. Most everyone that stops in talks about the money Boo will make in the oil fields. But then Henry Skiver says, "I can't see it," when I tell him that Floyd Bowman said Boo will make twenty dollars an hour starting out. "Shit, that Nesser boy wouldn't work in a pie factory." For a minute I get my hopes up, see all sorts of possible disasters happening once they hit Texas. Hell, I even picture Tina coming back with her head hanging down, asking me for a place to stay. Then Henry pulls out his little change purse and carefully counts out ten pennies for a cake, and I feel low again remembering the time she compared me to her dingbat cousin.

It looks like it's going to be a slow Tuesday, so I start breaking open the boxes that the Manker's man delivered yesterday.

I check everything against the yellow invoice, stamp prices on cans of Spam and Campbell's soup, and stock the bare spots on the shelves. I turn on the radio and listen to Miss Sally Flowers rattle on about everything she's grateful for this hot, sticky morning. That gets old real quick and I turn the station. The DJ puts on a Monkees' song, and I sing along to "Last Train to Clarksville" while I sweep the dust out the door and change the dirty fly ribbon that hangs over the kerosene stove in the back. All the time I'm piddling, I keep an eye on the gas pumps. Some people like to turn the handle back a gallon or two if they don't think I'm watching. Boo's one of the worst for pulling that kind of shit. He gets caught doing that down in Texas, they'll break his goddamn head for him.

Around noon, I'm getting ready to take a break and watch *As the World Turns* on the little TV I've got set up behind the candy case when I see Jake Lowry walking out of the holler past the church. He shuffles along with his hands crammed deep down inside his patched-up bibs like he's playing pocket pool with himself. As he crosses the road, he kicks at a busted beer bottle lying at the edge of the store lot. Most times I turn the TV off when I see someone coming because I don't like for people to know I watch soap operas, but I don't give a damn what Jake thinks. He never has played with a full deck all the time I've known him, and people say it's because he lived so long in the woods by himself back during WWII, hiding out from the draft. Right outside the door, he stops and spits a long string of tobacco juice in the gravel. The screen door slams behind him as he steps inside the store, and he jumps like someone just shoved a cob up his ass. He's the flightiest bastard I've ever seen.

Jake works the chew in his mouth, lays two arrowheads down carefully on the counter. I open the register and count out some change. Maude gives him forty cents for each one he finds, then she turns around and sells them to the Sinclair man for two dollars. He brings in five or six a week, sometimes more. I lay the money on the counter and Jake pushes a quarter back at me, like he always does. His dirty fingernails are long and cracked down the middle. I slide the glass door open on the meat case and lift out a roll of headcheese. He likes his cut thick, and I adjust the meat slicer. I try not to think about us both eating the same damn thing every day, and what that might mean to a head doctor.

I've been slicing meat so many years now I don't even bother with the scales anymore. I can hit it within a penny or two every time. After I wrap the gray meat in a sheet of butcher's paper and tape it shut, Jake sticks it in his pocket. He stands there working his chew, staring at the TV show. Neither one of us says a fucking word the whole time, but I'm used to that. Jake wouldn't say *shit* if he had a mouthful. I'm lighting a cigarette when Boo Nesser's car flies past the store and turns in at Tina's mother's house down the road. Suddenly, my headache breaks loose again, and I crack open another RC, pop a couple more aspirins.

As the World Turns is just going off when I hear car tires crunching on the gravel. A new Cadillac convertible pulls up to the gas pumps with a man and woman in the front seat. Jake leans back against the pop cooler and peers through the screen door. By the time I grab my oil rag, the woman's already out of the car and taking a picture of the store sign out by the road. It's just a rusty old Sinclair sign on a metal pole, but underneath the green dinosaur hangs a piece of plywood that says in big black letters WELCOME TO KNOCKEMSTIFF, OHIO. Maude spent a whole day in the back room painting the letters on, trying to get them right, but they're still crooked.

The man slides out from behind the wheel and stretches. He's maybe forty years old, tall and thin, wearing neat gray slacks and a white shirt. A gold chain hangs around his tan neck. He reminds me of one of those soap opera doctors, the way he smiles as he looks around. "So, this is Knockemstiff?" he says, waving his arm about slowly. The Cadillac has California license plates. We've had a few people drive through here from other states before, most of them lost, but never from that far off.

I follow the man's hand with my eyes, up the dirt lane lined with dusty trees that leads to the top of the holler, then down the patchy blacktop road that runs in front of the store and goes all the way over to Route 50. There's not a single soul moving about. "This is it," I say. I wad up the greasy rag in my hand.

"Don't seem to be much here," the man says. He takes a white handkerchief from his back pocket and pats his forehead.

"Well," I say, "there's a church over there." I point with my rag. "And up the road a ways is a bar. They call it Hap's. Right past it, there's another store, but they don't sell gas." I stop and think for a second. Behind me, I hear the woman's camera clicking, but I'm afraid to look her way. "We got a ball diamond just up there around the bend, but it's mostly houses, I guess. It's kinda spread out."

"Looks like it," the man says. He bends down and flicks a speck of dust off the top of his shiny shoe, then straightens back up. "Why the hell do they call it *Knockemstiff*?" he asks. "Seems like a pretty tough name for a place this quiet."

I sigh and reach in my pocket for a cigarette, but I've left my pack inside. I've probably been asked that question thirty or forty times since I started working for Maude, but I'm no storyteller. And the tale of how Knockemstiff got its name sounds stupid, even when the old-timers get loaded and tell it. But these people have come clear from California, and the man is expecting some kind of answer. "Not much of a story," I say. "Supposedly these two women got in a fight over a man up there in front of the church. One was the wife and the other was the girlfriend. The preacher heard one of them swear she was going to knock the other one stiff." I shrug and look at the man. "I guess the place hadn't been named yet. That all happened before I was born."

The man nods as I finish talking, and I turn to see the woman standing next to me now, writing something down in a little black notebook. "My wife's a photographer," he explains. "We've been driving across the country all summer, looking for places just like this to put in her book. It's been pretty exciting for her."

I pull my eyes away from the woman's made-up face. She's wearing white slacks and sandals and a soft flowered blouse. I wonder if the man is putting me on, making fun of me in front of his pretty wife. It's hard to imagine why someone would make a special trip just to take a picture of Knockemstiff, or put such a picture in a book, but then I've never been able to figure out why the government sent those VISTA guys here two years ago to help the kids out, either. I look down at the greasy rag in my hands. The pink polish on the woman's toenails is the same color as her lips. All of her parts match perfectly, and I try to remember if I've ever seen that before in real life.

"Did you know there's a place called Toad Suck?" the man says, smiling.

"That's a good name."

"It's in Alabama," he says. "Or Arkansas, I can't remember. Which is it, Charlotte?"

"Arkansas," the woman says. She's fiddling with her camera, taking another glass lens out of the leather bag hanging from her shoulder.

"It's hard to believe there's people that poor in this country," the man says. "Living in the richest nation in the world." He shakes his head and frowns, and though I don't figure he really gives a shit, I can't help but think that he sounds just like the VISTA man. I smile to myself and remember the first time Gordon Biddle stopped at the store in his short pants and floppy straw hat, looking for volunteers to help build a ball diamond. Someone had talked the paper mill in town into donating a little piece of flat land that sat at the edge of one of their timber stands. The boys from the holler worked like dogs for him all that summer, clearing the field of brush and rocks, smoothing over the rough spots with picks and shovels. Gordon paid more attention to them that one summer than most of their parents ever had. Once or twice a week, he'd load a bunch of them in his station wagon and take them swimming at the state park over by Hillsboro. Then one night he just packed up and left without even saying good-bye, and there was a lot of stupid talk about him and that Russell boy after that. Within a couple of weeks, the government sent another VISTA man, but that one, he was all business. That was just two years ago, but I noticed the other day that the green briars are already taking back the playground. The swing sets were already knocked over. It's no wonder poor people get a bad name.

The man coughs and I snap out of it. "Sorry," I say. "Did you want gas?"

Just then the woman squeals at her husband. "My God, Arthur, a chicken just walked into that house over there!" She's pointing at Whitey Ford's place right across the road from the store. Ever since his wife died back in the spring, the old man has kept his front door open, even at night. Animals and insects congregate there like fat people at a free dinner. Some people claim he's gone off the deep end, but Whitey says he likes the company. Hell, I can surely understand that. The woman takes a couple of steps forward, shoots some more pictures of the stray dogs curled on the front porch.

The man looks at me and grins. "She's a city girl."

I glance back at the store, wonder what Jake is up to inside. "Look, I got things to do," I tell the man. "Anything you need?"

The man says, "Yeah, anyplace we can get something to eat around here?"

"Well, not really. I got lunch meat and cheese. I could fix you-all a sandwich, if that's what you mean."

The man looks down at my dirty hands, and then glances at the store. "What about that bar you mentioned?"

I shake my head. "Hap don't serve no food. Besides, I don't think you'd want to take your wife in there." Just then the door squeaks opens and Jake tries to sneak out past us, his head hanging down like a whipped dog's. The woman wheels around at the sound and snaps his picture faster than a pheasant hunter getting off a shot.

Then she says to Jake in a loud voice, "Excuse me?" He hurries along, his face turned away from us. I wonder if I should stop her. He'll shit his pants if the woman keeps it up. "Excuse me," she says again, louder this time. Jake's practically going at a run by now. She motions to me and points. "That man," she says excitedly. "Could you ask him if I could take his photograph before he gets away?"

"I don't know, lady," I say. "Jake's kinda funny."

"Just one," she says. "He'd be perfect."

I toss the rag toward the door and yell for Jake. He freezes in his tracks at the edge of the store lot. I jog across the gravel and say to him in a low voice, "That lady wants to take your picture."

He looks at me with fear in his eyes, and then shoots a quick glance back at the California people. "I didn't do nothing," he says. His voice is shaky. Tobacco juice has stained his gray chin whiskers brown.

I see the round bulge of something in his pocket, and I figure he's probably got me for another can of pork and beans. "I know that," I say. "It's just what she does, Jake. She takes pictures of people."

He shakes his head. "I don't like that, Hank," he says. Then he starts off again. It's the first time in all these years I've ever heard him say my name.

I walk back over to the woman. By the look on her face, I can tell she's disappointed. "I didn't figure he'd do it," I say.

She shrugs, takes a photo of Jake's backside, and then turns to me. "What about you?" she asks. "Just a couple of pictures underneath that sign?" She steps a little closer and I get a faint whiff of her perfume. A trickle of sweat runs down her neck, and disappears beneath her silky blouse.

I look up and down the road, but I don't see any cars coming. The holler's dead, everything in it hypnotized by the noonday heat. "I don't know," I say. "I ain't much for pictures either." The last time I had one taken was in high school, right before the old man died. We drove into Meade on a Saturday, and he bought me a white shirt and one of those little clip-on ties at Elberfelds. All the way home he kept teasing me about looking like a preacher boy. That was the last good day we ever had together.

"Please?" the woman says.

Though I wish these people would just leave, I can't refuse the lady. "All right," I say, "if you hurry. I got work to do."

"It won't take but a minute," she says. We walk out to the sign by the edge of the road. She tells me exactly where to stand, and then she moves away a few feet. I see Jake glance back at us, and then slow down a little bit. Behind me, I hear a car coming. I turn and see Boo Nesser's green Ford pop up over the hill. "Christ," I say to myself, looking back at the woman, hoping she'll speed things up a little bit. But the car pulls up fast beside me and squeals to a stop on the asphalt. I stare straight ahead. "Okay," the woman says. "Say *Knockemstiff*."

"What?" I say. I push the hair out of my eyes. Standing in the sun, I'm starting to sweat out last night's Blue Ribbon, and I worry about the smell.

"She wants you to say *Knockemstiff*, you dumb shit," Boo says. He's got a red bandanna wrapped around his head, a little feather sticking up in the back. His head is hanging out the window, his big teeth as yellow as dandelion blooms in the bright light. Three or four big cardboard boxes are strapped to the top of the car with baling wire and rope. A table lamp is standing up in the backseat. Everything he and Tina own in the world, I think. Boo flicks a cigarette butt at me and laughs when I jump back. Though I won't go so far as to say I hate him, I guess I wouldn't mind if he dropped over dead right now.

"You know, like instead of *cheese*," the woman says. "Just try it."

"Okay," I say. Then I hear a door open on the Ford and Tina runs around the car and hops in the grass beside me. The girl doesn't have a backward bone in her body. She's wearing a tight pair of cutoff jeans and a baggy T-shirt she bought two weeks ago at the county fair for a dollar that says DO UNTO YOUR NEIGHBOR, THEN SPLIT. I know everything about her, and I wonder how long it will take me to forget that. "Do you care if I get in on this?" she asks the woman. "This might be my last chance to get my picture took with a dumb hillbilly." She smells like bacon grease and Ivory soap.

"Your last chance?" the woman says, looking up from the viewfinder. "What do you mean by that?" Her voice sounds a little aggravated at first, but then I see her look down at Tina's dirty bare feet and smile.

"Because me and Boo's headed for Texas," Tina says, "and we ain't coming back." Her arm brushes against mine, and I feel a jolt like electricity. "Ain't that right, baby?" My heart starts beating faster.

"That's right, sweetie," Boo says. Then he shuts the engine off. "We done outta this fuckin' place," he whoops.

The woman gives a little laugh and glances over at her husband. I turn and look, too. He's leaning against the car, his eyes fixed on Tina's ass. "Well, I sure don't blame you for that," the woman says to Boo, flashing him a smile. She raises the camera again and steadies herself. "Okay, ready? Say *Knockemstiff*."

"Knockemstiff!" Tina yells, so loud it seems to echo off the hills. Then she turns and punches me hard in the arm. "Come on, Hank, goddamn it, you didn't even try."

"All right," I say and nod at the camera. "One more time." Then we say it together—Knockemstiff—and it almost sounds like it means something. The woman squats down and shoots a couple more pictures. Tina giggles, and I try my best to smile, but my face can't seem to manage that right now. As I stand there, next to the woman that I covet, my head buzzes with all the things I want to tell her before she leaves, but I don't say a word. I might as well be out following my old man's ghost around in that orchard, afraid to kill a rabbit. And then I hear Boo yell, "Come on, Tina, it's time to go," and I can't even say good-bye. Instead, I lean back against one of the signposts and watch Jake's gray head start to sink over the other side of the hill.

That same night, at nine o'clock sharp, I take the money out of the cash register and stick it in the box. I figure I took in over a hundred dollars since morning. Maude never did come around, never even called on the phone to see how I was doing, and it's been another long fucking day. I sit out back beside my camper and watch the green hills slowly disappear as the last of the light fades away. After a while, I take my shoes off and pop a Blue Ribbon, light a cigarette.

Down the road Clarence starts up the same shit again with his old lady, and I wonder where Tina is tonight. I think about us putting on a show out front today for that California woman, and all those photographs that she took. I turn the beer up and suck the suds out of it, toss the empty over in the pile. Right before she left, the woman tried to hand me a couple dollars for my trouble, but instead I asked her to send me one of those pictures. "One with me and the girl," I told her, and she promised that she would. When it comes, I'll stick it up in the store through the day so that people can see it. And at night, I'll take it down.

HAIR'S FATE

WHEN PEOPLE IN TOWN SAID INBRED, WHAT THEY REALLY meant was lonely. Daniel liked to pretend that anyway. He needed the long hair. Without it, he was nothing but a creepy country stooge from Knockemstiff, Ohio—old-people glasses and acne sprouts and a bony chicken chest. You ever try to be someone like that? When you're fourteen, it's worse than being dead. And so when the old man sawed off Daniel's hair with a butcher knife, the same one his mom used to slice rings of red bologna and scrape the pig's jowl, he might as well have cut the boy's ugly head off, too.

The old man had caught Daniel playing Romeo in the smokehouse with Lucy, Daniel's little sister's carnival doll. Daniel was giving it to her good, making believe she was Gloria Hamlin, a snotty, bucktoothed cheerleader who'd spit chocolate milk on him last year in the school cafeteria. "Boy, that's Mary's doll," the old man said when he jerked the smokehouse door open. He said it matter-of-factly, like he was just telling his son that the radio was calling for rain, that the price of hogs was down again.

To make matters worse, Daniel couldn't quit, or even slow down. Trapped in the bright July sunlight pouring in through the open doorway, he was at that point in his fantasy where Gloria was begging him to split her in two with his big, hairy monster; his poor hand couldn't have stopped if the old man had chopped it off and thrown it to the dogs. With a shudder, he unloaded his jizz all over Lucy's plastic face, the crooked orange mouth, the bobbing blue eyes. Then, like an omen, a black wasp glided down from the rafters and landed gently on top of the doll's fake blond hair.

"That's Mary's doll," the old man repeated, his voice revving up this time, trembling with static. He stood there for a minute, looking down at the doll Daniel still clutched in his shaky hand. The wasp began struggling to pull itself loose from the sticky hair. "I always knew you was a retard," the old man said, reaching over and squashing the insect between two calloused fingers. Then he pursed his lips and shot a stream of brown tobacco juice on Daniel's bare feet, something he loved to do to all his family at impromptu times. "Now zip up and get rid of that goddamn thing before your sister gets hold of it," the old man said. "I'll take care of you later."

Stooped over with another disgrace, Daniel carried Lucy down to Black Run and threw her into the muddy water. He watched her float past the cable that marked their property line, then walked slowly back up through the field to the slab house. Maybe he was turning into a sex fiend like his uncle Carl, he thought. He pictured himself in the nuthouse on the hill over in Athens, sharing a padded cell with his crazy uncle, trading sick stories about the good old days, arguing over who gave the best blow job, Barbie or Ken.

For the rest of the afternoon, Daniel warily watched the old man strut around with a fifth of wine like the Prince of Knockemstiff, the kind of windbag who showed no mercy and killed blood relatives for an extra sack of corn. Finally, near suppertime, he called Daniel into the kitchen. The rest of the family was already gathered around the Formica table with the bent leg so they could benefit from the old man's royal blathering. Daniel's mom nervously polished one of her lard buckets and Toadie, the little brother, kept sticking his tongue on the fly ribbon that hung from the ceiling, while the sister, Mary, stood still as a tree in front of the window.

The old man walked in a circle around Daniel, scratching his chin and looking the boy over as if he were a prize shoat at the county fair. Finally he stopped and pronounced, "You need you a goddamn haircut, boy."

Daniel, his heart sinking like a stone, took a deep breath and resigned himself to the scissors his mom kept in the kitchen drawer. But then, in a surprise move, the old man whipped out the long knife instead and shoved his son down in a chair. "You goddamn move, I'll scalp you like an Injun," he said as he gathered up a long brown lock of Daniel's hair in his fist and began sawing close to the scalp. He was like that, the old man, full of mischief when everyone else was down.

It was like being in the electric chair, Daniel would think later, though without the pleasure of dying, or even a last meal. But with specks of his blood splattered all over the corn bread, and hair floating in the soup beans, who was hungry anyway?

Later that evening, Toadie skipped out to the rotten picnic table under the hickory tree where his older brother sat brooding over hair and hair's fate. All summer, Daniel had dreamed of stepping onto the school bus after Labor Day with his hair hanging down to his shoulders. The scene was as clear and vivid as a movie in his head, and now the old man had taken it away. "You look like a dern lightbulb," Toadie said, running a broken plastic comb through his own greasy locks.

"Shut your mouth," Daniel said.

"You was ugly and now you're real ugly," the little brother said.

"Want your ass kicked?"

"Mary wants her doll back," Toadie said, determined to rub it in.

"Tell her it ran away."

"That ain't the truth and you know it," Toadie said, though a crinkle creased his forehead as if he were trying to imagine it. "How's Lucy gonna run away?"

Daniel stared across the hills behind the house. The red sun was sinking like a giant fizzing bomb behind the Mitchell Cemetery, where hair continued to grow, undisturbed by butcher knives and old men. "She hitchhiked," he told his little brother.

That night, while lying in bed and listening to the old man cuss some rock-and-roll band playing on the *Ed Sullivan Show*, it suddenly occurred to Daniel that anyone, even he, could be a hitchhiker. He'd had it with hick hairdos and lard sandwiches and having to make up movies in his head while the old man hogged the TV. When Ed called the rock group out for an encore, Daniel heard the crash of a bottle against the wall. "Might as well watch niggers as listen to this shit," the old man yelled at the TV. The boy ran his hands slowly across his head, searching out each tiny gash that had been made with the knife. Then he rolled over and began planning his escape.

A FEW DAYS LATER, DANIEL WALKED TO ROUTE 50 AND stuck his thumb out. It wasn't long before a white semi speeding past suddenly downshifted to a stop, the air brakes screeching, the trailer bucking and hopping on the asphalt. The truck driver's name was Cowboy Roy. At least that was the name spelled out in ragged black electrical tape on the rusty doors of the cab. "I ain't really no cowboy," he blurted before the boy even got settled in the seat. Pulling back onto the highway, he went on to confess that he'd never actually been on a horse, either; that, in fact, he was allergic to horsehair. "Everyone's got their cross to bear, I reckon," the trucker said, pushing back the black ten-gallon hat that sat on top of his round, sweaty head.

Cowboy Roy was on his way home to Illinois. He was fat and wore tight coveralls that threatened to split open every time he hit a bump in the road. His feet were encased in pointy brown cowboy boots. A set of shiny spurs hung from the mirror. To make up for his allergy to horses, Cowboy Roy did other manly cowboy stuff, like drink cheap whiskey from a pint bottle and chew stringy tobacco and write songs in the tradition of Marty Robbins.

Daniel didn't say anything. He figured the man had as much right to call himself a cowboy as the movie stars on TV. The trucker rattled on about the best way to build a campfire in the rain. It suddenly occurred to Daniel that out here on the road you could be any damn thing you wanted to be. You could make up a new life story for every stranger who offered you a ride. You could be a Boy Scout without a single badge, a millionaire without a pot to piss in, a cowboy without a horse.

"So," Cowboy Roy finally said, "where'd you get that haircut? Cops do that to you?"

"Nah, my old man," Daniel said.

"Damn, he musta been highly ticked off," the trucker said. "What the dickens got him so riled up?"

Daniel hesitated, thinking of the day in the shed with Lucy, then finally said, "He caught me with his girlfriend."

Cowboy Roy gave a low whistle. "Well, that'd do it," he said. "But pap or no pap, I'd shoot a man down like a dog that scalped me like that."

"It weren't like I didn't want to."

"So you ran off instead?" the trucker asked.

"When I go back, I'll have hair clear to my knees," the boy vowed, staring out the dirty windshield.

Just as they crossed over into Indiana, Cowboy Roy gave Daniel a red snot rag to tie around his neck, just like the one that he wore. "So people will think we work the same spread," he explained. Then he handed the boy a harmonica to play while he sang a song he'd just thought up. Puffing out his cheeks, Daniel raised the mouth harp up to his lips, then noticed a thick glob of tobacco juice oozing from one of the reeds. "I don't know how to play," he told the trucker.

"Shoot, just blow on the damn thing," Cowboy Roy said. "You know how to blow, don't you?"

"Yeah, I guess so."

"I'll bet you do," the fat man said with a grin.

"What's the name of the song anyway?" the boy said, banging the harmonica on his knee, trying to knock the spit out of it.

"It don't have no name," the trucker said, "but it's the best dern love song I ever wrote."

They traveled across the bottom edge of Indiana, past sleepy cornfields and remodeled Indian mounds and small towns still decorated with sagging Fourth of July banners and painted rocks. Cowboy Roy broke out a pint of red-eye, and before long Daniel's head felt as fluffy as a paper cone of cotton candy. The trucker began talking a mile a minute about driving straight on through to Mexico. He said they could become bandits and hide out in a smoky cantina with a servant boy who would worship them in return for scraps off the table. He described young Miguel in minute detail, right down to the tiny purple birthmark on his lower stomach. Then he pulled a small plastic bottle from his coveralls and shook out some white tablets. "Here you go," Cowboy Roy said, handing Daniel two pills.

"What are these?" the boy said.

"Them's trucker's lifesavers. They keep you awake, make your dick hard as blacktop. Longhairs call 'em speed."

Daniel recalled once seeing a photo of an actual speed freak in Mrs. Kenney's health class at school. Her brother, a prison guard in Kentucky, had sent it to her. The teacher claimed the man was only thirty years old. His skin was drawn tight as a drum over his grinning face. "Once you start on that stuff, you're like one of those space comets that don't ever stop," the woman warned the class that day, as they passed around the picture of the pale stick with the brittle heart. Daniel looked down at the white pills the trucker had given him, then tossed them in his mouth and waited for takeoff.

Cowboy Roy was an independent trucker, but drove much of the time for a big slaughterhouse in Illinois, delivering meat throughout the tristate area. He'd seen enough filth to give up eating most flesh altogether. "It just breaks my heart to see some mom stick a hot dog in her baby's trap," he told Daniel. His favorite food now was pork and beans. "Eat 'em right out of the can," he said, "just like the cowboys do." He'd inherited a little spread, and as they crossed over into Illinois that evening, he invited Daniel to spend the night. "It gets pretty lonely at the ranch ever since Mom died," he said, his voice cracking just a little.

Daniel was surprised that the landscape didn't change after they left Ohio. He'd always thought of every other state as an exotic world, but so far everything he'd seen was as dull as a Lawrence Welk tuba special. In the meantime, though, the pills and whiskey turned him into a regular chatterbox, and before he could stop himself, he told Cowboy Roy the whole sad story of Lucy and the butcher knife.

"Sounds kinda kinky to me," the trucker said. He lit the butt of a skinny black cigar he'd stashed behind his ear, and blew a cloud of smoke in the boy's face.

"It woulda been down to my shoulders by the time school started," Daniel said, shivering with a speed rush.

"I never cared much for dolls myself," Cowboy Roy said. "Hell, they just lay there, you know what I mean?"

"My little cousin's got one that talks when you pull a string," the boy said. He rocked back and forth in the seat, unable to hold still.

"It's a shame they don't sell live ones," the man said, mashing his bloodshot eyeballs with his fist.

Eventually Daniel and the trucker dropped the trailer off in a potholed parking lot outside a warehouse on the edge of a small town. Then they drove on for another hour or so, and near dark, the trucker pulled down a long, secluded driveway lined with pine trees. He parked the semi in front of an ancient house trailer that had PONDEROSA spray-painted in big red letters across the front of it. "I got twelve acres here," the trucker told Daniel as they stomped through the weeds to the trailer. "We could put on a rodeo if we took the notion."

Stepping up on some cement blocks, he pushed a key in the

door and shoved it open. "It ain't no dude ranch, but it's good enough," he said, beckoning the boy inside. The trailer smelled like a closet full of bad times. All the windows were shut, and it must have been a hundred degrees inside. Black flies crawled on the walls. A flaky brown snakeskin was stretched out on the kitchen counter. Daniel looked around at the empty whiskey bottles and pork-and-beans cans lying on the floor. The shabbiness of the trailer suddenly choked him up, made him think of home.

He asked Cowboy Roy for another pill. "I can pay for it," Daniel said, reaching for some crumpled singles in the front pocket of his jeans. The sixteen dollars was all the money he had left from selling blackberries that summer. He'd picked them in the bottoms down past Pumpkin Center, then walked door to door all over Twin Township peddling them for thirty cents a quart.

"Shoot, pardner, your money ain't no good here," the trucker said. "What's mine is yours." Digging the bottle out of the side pocket of his coveralls, he uncapped it and gave Daniel two more pills, then flopped down on a sagging couch. "You think you could pull these boots off for me?" Cowboy Roy asked the boy. "My poor feet's killin' me."

Daniel got down on his knees in front of the truck driver and tugged both boots off. "How 'bout my socks, too?" Cowboy Roy said. Peeling the damp, dirty socks off, the boy was nearly knocked down by the rotten odor that sprang up from the wrinkled purple feet and filled the cramped room. The smell reminded him of the sick bucket his mom sat by the couch whenever the old man was on a binge.

"It sure is hot in here, ain't it?" the boy said, as he stood up and stepped away.

"Yeah, Mom screwed all the damn winders shut the first

year I went out on the road," Cowboy Roy said. "Poor old woman, she always got jittery when I was gone." Then he heaved himself up off the couch and stepped into the kitchen. "What we need is some cold beer."

The thought of any more alcohol combined with the smell of the trucker's feet made Daniel queasy. "Maybe later," he said. All his nerve endings felt exposed, the coating that covered them burned away by the speed. Even the light from the lamp hurt his eyes.

"Well, what about a shower?" the trucker yelled from the kitchen. Daniel could hear drawers sliding open, cupboards slamming shut. "That'd cool you off."

Walking into the bathroom, Daniel saw a shoot-'em-up paperback floating in the commode, its pages swollen with water. An old road atlas lay on the filthy blue linoleum. He hesitated, then locked the hollow door and took his clothes off. Pulling back the feed sack that served as a shower curtain, he saw that the tub was caked in hard gray scum. He tore some pages from the atlas, and covered the trucker's slime with the endless highways of America. There wasn't any soap, but he rinsed off in the cold spray anyway, patted himself dry with a stiff, bloody towel that hung from a nail on the wall. Then he put his clothes back on and walked out to the living room.

Cowboy Roy was sitting on the couch, a can of beer in his hand. He was grinning wildly at Daniel, baring his brown teeth like a dog. Uncapping the pill bottle, he threw several more tablets in his mouth and chased them down with the beer. "Look what I found," he said, reaching down and lifting a long blond wig delicately from a plastic bag on the floor.

"What the hell?" Daniel said, jumping back. He suddenly felt closed in, as if the room was a coffin, and the hair the trucker held in his hand the same as that which grew in the graves on the hill back home.

"Aw, come on," the truck driver said. "We're just fuckin' around here."

"Whose is that?" the boy asked.

"It was my mom's," Cowboy Roy explained. "But she don't need it no more. The cancer done ate a hole clean through her." He held the wig out to Daniel. "Go ahead, try it on."

Daniel took another step back. "No, I better not," he said.

"You was crying about not having no hair, wasn't you?" Cowboy Roy said. "I'm just tryin' to help you out is all."

"I don't know," the boy said. "Seems kinda weird."

"Son, your daddy caught you fuckin' a doll," Cowboy Roy said. "If that ain't weird, then nothing is."

Daniel ran his hand over the patchy stubble on his head. A cricket chirped from somewhere in the room. Glancing out the window, he saw the darkness settling over unfamiliar land. It amazed him to think that just that morning he'd slipped out of bed while his parents were still sleeping and now he was hundreds of miles from home. "Okay," he finally told the trucker.

"Now we're talking. Why walk around like that when you don't have to?" the fat man said, wiping the sweat from his bloated red face with the hairpiece. "Okay, just stand in front of that mirror and I'll help you put it on. I used to stick this thing on Mom all the time."

Daniel stepped over to the big oval mirror hanging from the paneled wall and shifted about nervously as Cowboy Roy set the musty-smelling wig on top of his head. "Hold still," he ordered the boy, working the elastic band of the hairpiece down over the boy's skull. "Got to make it fit right, don't we?"

the trucker said, looking over Daniel's shoulder and grinning at him in the mirror. The boy could feel the man's belly pressing up against him.

Finally, the trucker said, "Not bad. What you think?"

The long wig cascaded down Daniel's scrawny back, a tangle of big blond curls. "It's a little long, ain't it?" the boy said.

"Well, shoot, you just need a trim," the trucker said. "Stay right there." Cowboy Roy hurried into the kitchen and came back out with a jagged fillet knife. "I can't find no scissors, but this will do the job." He grabbed a length of the brittle hair in his stubby fingers. "Say about this much?" he asked the boy.

"Maybe I oughta do that," Daniel said.

"Just don't make no sudden moves," Cowboy Roy said.

"That's what my old man told me."

"Oh, yeah, I forgot," the trucker said. "Hell, I ain't gonna hurt you. This damn thing cost thirty dollars."

"That's good."

The trucker started in, chewing his chapped lips as he hacked off pieces of his dead mother's fancy wig and let them flutter to the floor. After a few minutes, he stepped away and slid the knife into the back pocket of his coveralls. He reached behind him for a pint bottle sitting on the end table next to the couch, his eyes never leaving the boy. As he unscrewed the cap, he said, "What you say now, pardner?"

Daniel stared into the mirror. The hair draped from his head like a thick curtain. He kept turning from side to side, looking at himself from different angles. No longer did he see the scabs on his scalp, the bony triangle of face, the acne flaming across his skin like a brushfire. "It does make a difference," he finally said, turning away from the mirror, his voice barely a whisper.

"Goddamn if it don't," Cowboy Roy said. "Hell, I bet there

ain't many dolls look so pretty." His face was flushed with heat, his body trembling. After steadying himself with a deep breath, he stepped closer and held out the bottle of whiskey. "C'mon, let's celebrate," he croaked.

Daniel tried to laugh, but that had always been too hard for him. He'd never had anything to celebrate, not once in his whole life. He took a small drink from the bottle, and as he handed it back, he felt the trucker's fat, sweaty hand touch his and linger there for a moment. And suddenly, Daniel knew that if he looked in the mirror again, he'd see the wig for what it really was. So instead, he closed his eyes.

PILLS

I WAS HIDING OUT IN FRANKIE JOHNSON'S CAR, A CANARY-yellow '69 Super Bee that could shit and get. We were on a spree, stealing anything we could get our hands on—tape players and car batteries, gasoline and beer. It was a day or two after my sixteenth birthday, and I hadn't been home in a week. And even though my old man was telling everyone around Knockemstiff that he hoped I was dead, he kept driving up and down the township roads with his head out the window looking for me like I was one of his lost coonhounds.

Frankie kept saying that three hundred dollars would get us to California, but the only person we knew who had anything worth that much money was Wanda Wipert. Depending on who she was fucking at the time, a man could end up sleeping at the bottom of the Dynamite Hole with trash fish and bald tires for ripping Wanda off. Besides that, my old man's place was right across the road from her house. "No way," I said. Even talking about it gave me the willies.

"Fuck 'em," Frankie said. "Shit, Bobby, we'll be three thousand miles away."

We broke in through the bathroom window. Pressed into the gray scum of the tub, our boot prints looked like those fossil feet frozen in rocks that my crazy cousins said the Devil had planted all over the world to trick people into believing that we came from frog shit and monkeys. There was a little radio next to the sink playing one of the country music stations. The DJ was announcing a sale on Thanksgiving turkeys at the Big Bear. A pair of red panties was balled up on the linoleum floor, and Frankie stuffed them into the back pocket of his coveralls. "Let's don't be fuckin' around here," I whispered. Every creak of the old house sounded like a gunshot to me.

The little meat freezer was in the hallway next to the bedroom door. Inside we found four bottles of black beauties—pharmaceutical speed—hidden under a quart of frozen strawberries and a Barbie doll still in the box. The pills were wrapped in a sheet of bloody butcher's paper that had CHUCKIE'S HOG BRAINS writ on it with a blue crayon. Somebody had already eaten the brains.

Wanda tended bar at Hap's and sold the black beauties on the side. The hilljacks loved them because a three-dollar capsule made it possible to drink four times as much and still miss the telephone poles on the way home. She had a whole posse of big girls that she carted around southern Ohio to the fat doctors. To get a prescription of black beauties, all they had to do was stand on the scales and let the nurse take their blood pressure. Wanda bribed the women with cheap tennis shoes from the Woolworth's and Rax Roast Beef sandwiches and Dairy Queen milk shakes. My older sister, Jeanette, was one of her regulars. The only time I ever saw her happy was after one of those trips with Wanda to cop a 'script. She always came back with mustard stains on her good blouse and something sweet for her two illegits.

"Maybe we oughta leave one bottle," I said.

"No way, Bobby," Frankie said. "We use our heads, these babies will get us clear to goddamn San Francisco."

"How long will it take to get there?"

"Five days," he said, shoving all four bottles deep down into his front pockets.

Leaving out the back door, we climbed up over Slate Hill and through the woods toward Foggy Moor. That's where we'd stashed the Super Bee. The moon rose up behind us like a flat, shiny skull. We had to fight our way through the brush and briars for two miles, but at least nobody would be able to say they'd seen us in the holler that night.

Four bottles of black beauties—240 pills—was enough rocket fuel to send a trash can to Mars. The pills still had frost on them when Frankie opened the first bottle and handed me two. Our plan was to eat just a couple, and then head west on Route 50 after we sold the rest in town. Within forty-five minutes my heart was ticking like a live bomb. By midnight I was chewing holes in my tongue listening to Frankie obsess about having sex with movie stars. "What about it, Bobby?" he finally asked me. "What would you do to her?"

Frankie had been listing all the stuff he wanted to do to Ali McGraw. I'd known him my whole life, but the part about the ax handle took me by surprise. I'd never been with a woman, and I was still trying to figure out if such a thing was even possible. "Shit, I don't know," I finally said with a shrug.

He fired up another cigarette off the one he was smoking. "Did you get off?" he asked, looking over at me.

"Yeah," I said. "Why?"

"I don't know, man. You just seem out of it."

"Look, I'm thinking maybe we should take them pills back, Frankie," I said. "I mean, if Wanda finds out—"

"Are you fuckin' nuts?" he said. He uncapped the bottle and handed me a couple more of the black capsules. "You're just comin' down, Bobby, that's all."

He was right—two more made all the difference. Within a few minutes, a great happiness surged up inside of me as I thought of running away to California. Suddenly, I knew that all the lousy, fucked-up things that kept happening in my life would never happen again. I remembered the last time my old man had went crazy on us, all because my mother had fixed him oatmeal instead of eggs for his breakfast. I began to talk and found that I couldn't stop. While Frankie drove around the township in circles that night, I told him all the secrets in my house, every single rotten thing that my old man had ever done to us. And though, in a stupid way, I felt like a fucking rat the more I blabbed, by the time the sun came up the next morning, it seemed as if all the shame and fear I'd ever carried inside of me was burned away like a pile of dead leaves.

WE RAN OVER THE CHICKEN THREE DAYS AFTER WE STOLE the pills. It came out of nowhere. I was at the height of my powers then. Eat twenty-five black beauties in three days and you will know what I'm talking about. "Fuck!" I yelled when I heard it thump against the car. Frankie slammed on the brakes and the car skidded to a stop. I jumped out. The chicken was smashed against the grill, its neck broken. I pulled it gently away from the chrome and held it up by its bumpy yellow feet. A glob of blood as fat and round as a red pearl hung on the end of its busted beak.

Climbing out of the car, Frankie said, "How'd that get

there?" He checked the front grill, wiped it off with his coat sleeve. Then he got down on his knees and looked underneath for damage. He loved that Super Bee. "Goddamn chicken," I heard him say.

"I can save it," I said.

Frankie stood up and frowned at me, pressed a finger against the side of his nose and blew snot all over his work boots. "It's dead, Bobby." He rubbed the toe of each shoe against the legs of his greasy coveralls while chewing the inside of his mouth as if it was a big soft seed. His pupils shone like tiny headlights in the dusk.

"I can save it," I repeated. I held the bird close to my chest, felt its warmth slowly slipping away in the cold wind blowing across the flat fields. The farmers had already picked the harvest. Two-inch stubble covered the landscape. Even the highway was empty. I stroked the chicken's tiny head with my thumb. "Pop the trunk," I said. Then I wrapped the body in my flannel shirt and laid it gently on top of a spare tire.

LATER THAT SAME NIGHT, I LOST MY CHERRY TO A GIRL with razor-thin lips who kept telling me to hurry up. Her name was Teabottom. We first saw her coming out of Penrod's Grocery in Nipgen carrying a carton of milk. Her red frizzy hair looked like a bush burning atop her head. She was wearing a ragged blue work shirt and grimy plastic sandals. Her feet were purple from the cold. A little leather purse hung from a dirty string around her neck. "Hey, baby!" Frankie yelled as he whipped the car into the gravel lot and cut her off.

We worked out a trade, and she climbed in the backseat. Frankie flipped a coin, and I went first. From everything I'd seen in the movies, I thought I should hold her tenderly, but she was all business. She pulled her shirt up over her head so I couldn't kiss her. The carton of milk busted in the floorboards and sloshed on my feet. I might as well have been in a barn-yard.

"Damn, she ain't no Ali McGraw, but I wish I had that fuckin' ax handle now," Frankie said to me the second time he climbed over the seat. Because of the speed, we couldn't get enough. We tried to wear her out, mostly because of the disdainful way she looked at us. But nothing we did made any difference to her as long as we handed her two more pills every time we took a turn. She stuck all of them in her change purse.

The third time I went for it, I asked her about the milk. My socks were soaked with it. "It was for my baby, dumbass," she said. She was smoking a cigarette, bitching about being sore.

"You got a baby?" I said.

"What, you hard of hearing too?"

"Well, where is it now?"

"Don't worry about it," she told me, holding out her hand. I laid two pills in her palm, and she spread herself down on the seat with a groan. But I couldn't stop thinking about her baby, and wondering who was taking care of it while Frankie and me tried to screw her brains out. I kept imagining all kinds of horrible, fucked-up things happening to it. When I finally gave up and climbed off of her, she cupped some of the spilled milk from the floor into her hand and poured it over her crotch. She didn't even bother pulling her jeans back on anymore.

Toward morning, as I drove us along a gravel road, I thought I heard Frankie telling the Teabottom girl that he would take her to Nashville as soon as he could get rid of me. But when I turned the radio down, all I could hear was the steady squeak of the seat behind me. I turned around in the seat, saw him hovering over the top of the girl with his eyes shut. "Frankie?" I asked.

"What?"

"What about California, man?" I asked. We hadn't left the county yet, hadn't sold a single pill.

"Jesus Christ, Bobby, not now."

When we finally let her out, Teabottom stumbled bow-legged to her trailer through a yard strewn with rusty car parts and old empty dog boxes. We sat in the Super Bee watching numbly as she stepped up on some wobbly cement blocks and went inside. A light popped on, then off again. I lit a cigarette and pulled another black beauty from the stash I had in my coat pocket. "My dick feels like a goddamn snappin' turtle's been chewing on it," Frankie said. Then he backed out of the driveway, burned a patch of rubber all the way through first gear. Above us, the black sky slowly turned into a gray waxen sea.

B Y THE END OF THE FIFTH DAY, WE WERE FRIED. NOW THE speed was like water running through our veins, and we couldn't get off anymore. Our throats had turned to leather from cigarettes and talk; our gums bled and our jaws ached from grinding our teeth together. Frankie kept whispering to a beer can that he held in his hand like a microphone, and I had struggled off and on all that day to convince myself that it wasn't talking back to him. And in the backseat, the spilled milk had soured and filled the car with rotten fumes that kept reminding me of Teabottom's little baby. "What about California, you fuck?" I finally said. "Shit, we coulda been there by now."

He sighed and whispered one more time to the can, then

tossed it out the window. "Hey, Bobby," he said, "you can go anytime you want. I ain't stopping you."

A few minutes later, we pulled into Train Lane, a rutted farm road that divided two cornfields on the edge of Knockemstiff. It didn't matter how many miles we traveled by day, we always ended up back in the holler at night, though I was scared shitless that we'd run into Wanda Wipert or, even worse, my old man. At the turnaround at the end of the lane, we parked beside an illegal dump, piled high with bags of trash and busted chairs and cast-off refrigerators. The sun was sinking with a purple glow behind the Mitchell Flats. The DJ announced the sale on Thanksgiving turkeys again.

"Jesus," I said, "how many fuckin' Thanksgivings are they having this year?"

Frankie shut the engine off and sat staring straight ahead for a few minutes. Then he jerked the keys from the ignition and stepped out of the car. I watched him hunt through the trash, throwing boards and paper off to the side. He found an old tire and rolled it out into the middle of the road. As he bent down and started stuffing the inside of it with paper and cardboard, I opened the glove box and grabbed one of the two bottles of black beauties we had left. I slipped the speed in the top of my sock and got out of the car. "What you doing, man?" I asked him.

He was holding his lighter to some of the damp paper, trying to get it to ignite. "I'm fuckin' cold, and I'm fuckin' hungry," he croaked. We both watched as a tiny flame began to grow inside the tire. "When you figure was the last time we ate?"

"I don't know," I said.

"It's been a week. At least a week, right?"

"Yeah," I said. "Maybe so."

Walking to the back of the car, Frankie opened the trunk and lifted the chicken out. My shirt was still wrapped around it like a shroud. "Oh, shit," I said. I fumbled for the last pill I had in my coat pocket and bit it open. "Just give me a minute here, man," I said, swallowing the bitter powder. "Maybe I can still do something."

Frankie shook his head. "You want your shirt back?" he asked. He was swinging the chicken back and forth by its feet as if he was trying to hypnotize me.

"No," I said. "Well, yeah, I guess so."

"Here, hold this, just for a minute." He handed me the stiff bird. Then he began digging through the trash again, finally pulling a broken stake out of the pile. "This'll work," he said to himself. Taking the chicken from me, he set it on the ground, and pressed his foot on its neck.

"What are you doing?" I said as I took off my coat and put my shirt back on.

"Watch," he said. And with one quick motion, he bent down and rammed the stake up the chicken's ass until the point broke through the breast with a crunchy sound.

"Goddamn it," I cried. I was so worthless I'd forgotten all about it, and now nobody could bring the chicken back to life. Then another thought occurred to me. "You're not going to screw that, are you?" I asked him. "Because I'll tell you right now, Frankie, I won't allow it."

"I hadn't thought of that," he said, "but no, I'm gonna eat the fuckin' thing." Then he lifted the chicken up and carried it toward the fire. One of the bird's eyes was open, staring at me blankly. A thin strand of blue intestines hung from the tip of the stake.

The tire was blazing now, the thick black smoke funneling

into the night. The smell of the burning rubber started to make me sick. I stood back and watched as Frankie held the carcass over the edge of the flames. The feathers curled and melted and disappeared. "Ain't you even gonna gut it?" I said, stepping closer.

He looked back at me and showed his teeth. "Just got to cook it," he gagged. He pulled Wanda's red panties from his pocket and held them over his face. The chicken began to grow soft, and started to slide off the end of the stick, but Frankie righted it just in time. The skin sizzled and smoked and started to turn black. Drops of fat began to splatter into the fire. The feet shriveled up and fell into the flames.

Without another word, I stepped across the drainage ditch and out into the soft barren field. I pulled the bottle of pills out of my sock, stuck them in my pocket. Route 50 was two miles away, and I started walking toward it. Mud stuck to my boots like wet concrete, and every few steps I had to stop to shake it off. Looking up, I saw the red blinking lights of an airliner, miles above me, heading west. I'd never been on a plane, but I imagined big-shot bastards on vacation, movie stars with beautiful lives. I wondered if they could see the glow of Frankie's fire from up there. I wondered what they would think of us.

GIGANTHOMACHY

IT HAD RAINED HARD DURING THE NIGHT, AND IN THE morning everything along the fence line was bright wet green except for that brown anthill. Even though we'd flattened the shit out of it just the week before, the damn thing was already the size of a bushel basket again. It was as if we'd never been there. Christ, they'd even buried the concrete block that William had left standing as a monument to their war dead.

"They're taunting us," William said, staring down at the ants gliding about on top of the soggy mound, repairing storm damage, oblivious to us, their mortal enemies.

"What," I said, "they're just bugs." William made a big deal out of everything. The whole world was out to get him, even the milkweed and the tumblebugs. His father, Mr. Jenkins, was the cause of it all. There were nine kinds of hell raised over at their house every night. The old man was some kind of maniac, and William walked around with a bitter scowl and a constant migraine. Before he moved in next door, I thought only old people got headaches. He was always getting me to steal some of my mom's aspirins for him, and then he sucked on them like hard candy, trying to make each one last as long as possible. Living with my mother was no picnic, but compared to what William and his sister, Lucy, had to go through, I was, as my uncle Clarence always put it, shittin' in high cotton.

"Did you bring the matches?" he asked. Yesterday William had finally agreed that if I brought the fire, we could kill Vietcong this week. My mom and I watched bits of the war on TV every night, and I had waited all goddamn summer to wipe out a Communist village.

I pulled the box of blue kitchen matches out of my pocket, and he ran to retrieve the empty bleach bottle he'd stashed in a clump of horseweeds that grew along the sagging fence. "We gotta be careful," he said, glancing back at his house. "The old man's on the warpath again."

"Jesus, don't that guy ever let up?" I said. The bruises on William's skinny arms were the color of a bum banana. All my life I'd wished for a father, but living next to Mr. Jenkins was making me have second thoughts. Mine had skipped out on my mom before I was born, and I'd always been ashamed of that. But maybe I'd lucked out after all.

"Light it," he commanded, ignoring me. Ramming a long stick in the mouth of the bleach bottle, he held it over the fence. I struck a match and held the flame close to the bottom of the jug until it caught. Then, swinging the stick around, William positioned the melting bottle directly over the anthill. Sizzling drops of white plastic began raining down on the tiny red ants like a firestorm.

"Look, Theodore," he said casually, "let's forget that Vietnam crap."

"But you said we could—"

"I can't stand it," he coughed. "It's all you ever talk about." Poisonous fumes were already swirling around his sweaty face. He waved his hand like a handkerchief, trying to fan the plastic smoke away.

"Fuck you," I said. "Find someone else to boss around." I was the only kid in Knockemstiff who would even talk to him, and that was just because my mom kept insisting that I play the good neighbor. Anytime I pointed out to her that William treated me like shit, she'd look up from whatever she was do- ing and say, "Teddy, you have no idea what goes on over there. Like I said, just keep *pretending* that William's your friend, and before you know it, he will be."

Maybe the reason my mother loved pretending so much was that she had such a hard life. When I was still a baby, she began working at the meatpacking plant in Greenfield, jam- ming bloody hog bones into cardboard boxes all day. She walked around smelling of pork, her knuckles swollen with tiny infected cuts. Over the years, she slowly become a devout dreamer, hooked on a special kind of make-believe that she made me promise not to talk about. She was always searching for my next persona, mostly in the cheap detective magazines she borrowed from Maude Speakman and read religiously every night before going to bed.

The first time it happened, she'd been telling me about Richard Speck over dinner, going into detail about the eight dead nurses while we ate bologna sandwiches and potato chips. She made it sound scary, but by bedtime I'd forgotten all about him. Then she came in and sat down on the side of my bed, drew tattoos on my arms with a ballpoint pen, handed me a pair of scissors. "Look, Teddy," she said, "I need you to do something for me."

"What's that?"

"Remember that Speck guy we talked about?" she said.

"The creepy killer?"

"That's him," she said. "Now what I want you to do is come in my bedroom and play like you're him. Just for a minute."

"How do I do that, Mom?"

"I don't know. Just spit on the floor maybe, talk like a drunken sailor," she said. "Hurt me, but don't really hurt me."

Other than the black pills she sometimes got off her sister, Wanda, fear seemed to be the only thing that made my mother feel alive. And because I wanted so much for her to be happy, I became a master at scaring the bejesus out of her. Albert De-Salvo was her favorite psycho, and she had a picture of him taped inside her closet. Sometimes, if she'd had a really bad day, I'd go outside and cut a hole through a window screen, then slip in and tie a fancy knot around her neck with a pair of her panty hose, all the while confessing that I was the *real* Boston Strangler.

In the beginning, before I got good at it, she was always giving me advice, always pointing out little ways in which I could better become somebody else. "You need to work on that accent," she'd say, or "Good Lord, Teddy, I could hear you coming from a mile away that time." So with my mother, fantasizing that William was my friend was no big deal, just another game to her. I stuck the box of matches in my pocket and turned to go home.

"Hold up, Theodore," William said. "What if we say they're giants?" He was standing with his feet spread apart, swinging the burning bleach bottle back and forth like an incense pot.

I looked down at the terrified ants fleeing their fortress.

Last week he'd insisted that they were African pygmies, talked me into playing Cheetah to his Tarzan. Now this. "Well," I said, "there's all kinds of giants. King Kong, Colossal Man, maybe . . ."

"For Christ's sakes, Theodore," he said, "this is serious business. These are fucking giants planning on taking over the world, not stupid movie monsters."

"So what are we then?" I asked hopefully. "Marines?"

"Marines?" he snorted. "What's a fuckin' jarhead going to do against a horde of giants?" I watched him look up at the sun and squint. "I know," he finally said. "We're gods. Only a god can stop something this big."

I looked down at William's feet. Crooked toes were poking through the ends of his rotten tennis shoes. The scars on his legs glistened like snakeskin in the morning light. Gods? He was the closest thing to a dead person that I'd ever played with. "Whatever," I said, giving in. "Gods. Giants. Giant ants."

He smiled, then coughed again. "I saw that Hiroshima on TV one time," he said, raising the bottle higher to get more of a splatter effect. "It looked just like this."

"Bullshit," I protested. "That was an atom bomb."

"So? What's your point?" he asked, staring at me through his thick dirty glasses.

"Well, this stuff—this stuff is more like napalm," I said. "Like what they use over in *Vietnam*." The jug was frothing now, like a volcano. Ants were burning to death all around us. I imagined their pitiful screeches. They smelled like little whiffs of burned popcorn.

"Jesus," William yelled, "there you go again!" He cocked the stick back as if he were going to sling the bottle on me. His whole body was quivering. A drop of sputtering plastic landed on his forehead, but he never flinched.

The last time he got excited like this, he chopped himself in the leg with a hoe, all because I refused to admit that my blue marble was really his green one. "Okay," I said, giving in again. "Then can we at least say that the smoke is—"

"Fallout!" he yelled. "Radioactive fallout. Yeah, that's what turned the ants into giants in the first place. See, Theodore, you're not so dumb."

Just then, Lucy came tearing out of the house. She was wearing William's fake army helmet and her cowgirl outfit, the one with the short sequined skirt. "He's got Mother trapped in the basement!" she panted. "I think he's killed her this time."

William looked grimly toward the house. "Good," he said. "Maybe he'll kill us all. We'd be better off." Last Christmas, right after they moved in, Mr. Jenkins beat his wife so bad that her left eye still drooped like a wilted blue blossom. I'd seen her a few times, wrapped in a sheet, staring out the kitchen window. She reminded me of the rocking-chair hag in *Psycho*, my mom's favorite movie.

"Hey, shithead," Lucy said to me, "you're not stepping over the line, are you?" Nobody was allowed on their property, especially me. My mom had called the sheriff on Mr. Jenkins a hundred times, but the fat deputies didn't want to get involved. They wouldn't even climb out of the cruiser anymore, just turned on the flashing light as they sped on through the holler.

William and I both looked down to make sure my feet were legal. Lucy was like the secret police. She had a mouth that wouldn't quit. The last time she'd ratted her brother out, you could hear his screams all the way to Foggy Moor. "Go spy on someone else," he told her.

"Just checking," she said, tossing the toy helmet to the

ground. Then she took off and did a flip that made her skirt go over her head. She was twelve, practically a grown woman to a nine-year-old. I could see her crack pressed tight against her white underwear. It looked like the knot in a tree. I wanted to fuck her, though I wasn't sure what fucking actually entailed. I just knew my mom did a lot of it. Every kid on the school bus said so.

"Dickweed," Lucy called out to me when she landed.

"Funny," I said, feeling my face begin to heat up.

"Cock breath," she yipped, kicking the toy helmet across the yard. The girl knew cuss words my mom's boyfriends had never even dreamed of.

"Lucy," William said, "leave Theodore alone! You're just jealous because I got a friend and you don't." Friend? It was the first time William had ever hinted that I was anything but his dumb puppet. Maybe my mom was right; perhaps all you had to do was pretend something was true and then someday it would be, no matter how fantastic, no matter how fucked up.

Just then a scream erupted from inside the house, followed by a loud crash. When William saw his sister start running toward the porch, he turned and handed me the stick. "Here," he said. "I better get in there. Aim for their heads."

"Wait, William," I blurted out. I stood there trying to think of something brave to say, but we both knew that I was scared shitless of his father. He cocked his head and looked at me impatiently. "Is there anything I can do?" I finally said.

"Theodore," William said, his face suddenly breaking into a crazy grin, "we're gods, remember? Shit, we can do anything." Then he turned and charged bravely at the house, pushing Lucy out of the way and disappearing through the back door.

All of the ants were dead. William had destroyed the entire

colony once again. As I started across the yard, my mother and some guy with fat sideburns pulled in our driveway in a homemade convertible. She was always bumming lifts from the people that she worked with at the hog plant. He was steering the car with one hand, grabbing at my mom's tit with the other. They were both laughing. When she looked up and saw me walking toward them carrying the charred stick like a smoking rifle, she pulled her blouse back down and waved wildly in my direction. Then, jumping out of the car, she gave her ride a peck on the cheek and ran inside the house.

Later that night, my mother told me again that I looked just like my father, and I wondered if that was make-believe too. She was lying on the bed in her silk robe, the scent of her perfume filling the hot room with flowers. Reaching over, she turned down the lamp that sat on the nightstand. Then she tilted her head back, and taking my hand in hers, guided the kitchen knife to her soft throat. "Okay," she whispered, closing her eyes, "who do you want to be tonight?"

Her moist pale skin glowed in the dim light, and a moth fluttered madly against the rusty window screen. I could feel her body trembling against the thin sharp blade. Outside, a thousand throbbing crickets urged me on, but I stood there a long time trying to decide. "Teddy," I finally said, pretending it was true. "I just want to be Teddy."

SCHOTT'S BRIDGE

NETTIE RUSSELL DIED IN THE SPRING, AND LEFT HER GRAND-son, Todd, an old Ford Fairlane and a Maxwell House coffee jar with two thousand dollars in it, a fair sum of money in 1973. Her only daughter, Marlene, had been a wild girl who had tossed her life away one snowy night when Todd was just two years old. A sheriff's deputy had found her in the backseat of a car at the edge of Harry Frey's orchard with a strange man from town lying on top of her, both of them stiff and blue and puffed up like toads from carbon monoxide. And since none of Marlene's boyfriends had the nuts to step up at the funeral and offer to help out with the orphaned boy, not even after a special plea from the preacher, Nettie had had no choice but to raise him.

When she handed over the inheritance, just a few hours before she took her last, wheezy breath, Nettie told her grand-son, "Toddy, you never did belong here. You take this, and you go somewhere else before you get hurt." He had just turned nineteen, and everyone in the holler had always joked that he had too much sugar in him for a boy. For several years, he had dreamed of moving away and selling real estate, maybe working in a bank. The fantasy of someday coming back to Knockemstiff dressed in a shiny burgundy suit and carrying a leather briefcase was one that had kept both him and his grandmother going during the last weeks of her long illness.

He should have headed for town as soon as she handed over the keys and the money, but Todd discovered that he was afraid of leaving the holler, even if it was bad. He kept stalling, hanging around the county, and within a month of the old lady's passing, he and Frankie Johnson moved into a fish camp that sat on the high side of Paint Creek. People couldn't figure it out. Frankie was rough as a cob and liked the splittails; Todd talked like a prissy girl in a beauty pageant and walked on his toes like his feet were full of glass.

Though they had known each other all their lives, they didn't start running together until one night after a beer party over by Copperas Mountain. Todd had been sleeping in the Fairlane ever since his grandmother's funeral, riding around listening to love songs on the radio and wishing his uncle Claude would get colon cancer. As soon as they'd returned from the cemetery, Claude had pitched Todd's clothes out into the muddy yard and told him to hit the road. "Mom wouldn't let me kick you out when she was alive, but she can't stop me now," he told his nephew. Except for the ghost he'd seen at his grandmother's headstone, Todd hadn't spoken to a soul in three weeks. He was just looking for a safe place to park for the night when he came upon the beer party. Loneliness always got him into trouble quicker than anything, and he knew that, but he pulled over and shut off the engine anyway.

He sat down under the canopy of a willow tree a good ways off from the bonfire and listened to the laughter and the wild talk. Nobody invited him over, but he didn't expect them to. People in the holler, especially the men, treated him with contempt at best. Tonight though, after the keg went dry, Frankie Johnson walked over and sat down on a log near him. "You got any money, Russell?" Frankie asked.

Todd thought for a moment. Though Frankie had never been what you'd call friendly, at least he'd left him alone when the others cussed him or chased him down the road throwing rocks. "Little bit," Todd said warily.

"Why don't we go into town and get some breakfast?" Frankie said. He looked off when he said it, like he was ashamed. "They say that Frisch's Big Boy is open all night now."

"Why?"

Frankie let out a sigh. He picked up a rock and squeezed it, then pitched it into some weeds. "I'm hungry, that's why," he said.

A car wreck had left Frankie with a long purple scar that ran down the side of his face like a crack in an egg, but Todd could still remember when he'd been a handsome man. Todd looked over at him, chewed his lower lip, considered the dangers and the possibilities. The possibilities won out. "Okay," he said.

A few of the drunks around the fire hooted when they saw Frankie start to climb into the old Fairlane. Todd was afraid there might be some trouble, but Frankie just flipped them the bird and settled back in the seat. Someone threw a beer bottle as they were turning around in the dirt lane, and it bounced off the fender. "Stupid sonsabitches," Frankie muttered. Then he closed his eyes and snored all the way to town. His rotten breath filled the front seat. Todd studied the raised scar in the headlights of oncoming cars and fought the desire to run his finger over it. He wondered if Frankie knew about the two thousand dollars.

As he ate his breakfast at Frisch's Big Boy, Frankie told Todd that the only thing he'd ever loved in his life was a yellow '69 Super Bee that he'd owned when he was seventeen. "I remember that car," Todd said.

Frankie smiled, stuffed some more egg into his mouth. "Everybody knew my Super Bee," he said. "Sonofabitch would fly. By God, I ever get a chance, I'll have another one just like it."

"Ain't that the one you wrecked?" Todd said.

Frankie stopped chewing and nodded. "Worst day of my life so far," he said. "Had some bitch call me Frankenstein the other night." Three years ago, he had missed the curve at Pumpkin Center, and when the Super Bee smashed into a telephone pole, he went face-first through the windshield. Everything might have turned out okay, but he was in the middle of a damn good binge, and he drank three more days before someone finally took him to the hospital to see about getting his face sewn up. By then, everything was starting to heal over, and there wasn't any way that the doctor could pull the big gash closer together. He told Frankie it was a miracle he hadn't bled clear out.

When Frankie paused to butter some toast, Todd started talking about his grandmother's slow death in the back room of the house. Uncle Claude had stopped by every day to see if she was dead yet, kept complaining that the smell was going to keep him from finding a buyer for the place once she was gone. Todd did okay until he tried to describe what it felt like when she took her last, shallow breath. "She was the only mother I ever had," he tried to say, but the words came out all garbled and snotty. Frankie put down his fork and handed

Todd a napkin from the dispenser. Then he stared out the window and picked at his teeth until Todd got up and paid the bill. They slept in the car that night, and early the next morning they bought three bottles of Thunderbird at Gray's Drugstore. By that afternoon, drunk and half sick, they were looking for a permanent place to stay.

The fish camp they rented was just two moldy rooms and a screened-in porch. They got it cheap from an old widow in town named Fletcher because it had no plumbing or electric. She told them her husband used to take his whores there on the weekends. "I oughta burn the damn place down, but I need the income," she said when she handed Todd the key. There was a rusted-out coal stove in one corner of the big room that housed black wasps in the summer and leaked black smoke in the winter. Somebody had drawn a life-size stick family on the wall with crayons. All the faded figures had blood pouring from their mouths. Even the dog or cat or whatever it was supposed to be was puking red. Out back was an old well lined with slimy green rocks where they could draw a bucket of water, but it tasted like gasoline. They never drank it, but sometimes Frankie liked to soak his rotten feet in it.

Neither one of them was much for work; so a couple of weeks after they moved in together, they bought a hundred hits of strawberry mescaline for ninety dollars. They ate a few and sold the rest, then bought another batch. Frankie knew lots of people, most of them bad. Todd handled the money and was enterprising in his own small way, but he was also careful. He worked it out so they made just enough to pay the rent, buy some lunch meat and bread, and keep Frankie supplied with cheap wine.

He hid the coffee jar filled with his inheritance behind a rock in the well. His brown hair grew long, and he cut a notch in the doorframe every time he took a trip. He watched the stick family move around on the wall and kill one another over and over. Within a few months he calculated he'd been completely out of his mind more than a hundred times. There were days when he had a hard time remembering his name. Sometimes he worried that he'd forget where he'd hid the coffee jar, and he'd go check on it. Frankie started walking around with a .22 pistol stuck down in his pants. "We gotta protect our empire," he said whenever Todd complained about the gun.

The fish camp overlooked Schott's Bridge, the easiest way in or out of the holler. Todd liked to sit on the porch, watch the cars pass over Paint Creek, and listen to the rumble of the tires on the heavy wooden planks. He still daydreamed about leaving. Once in a while, on hot days, they would walk down to the bridge to soak in the shallow riffles and hunt for pop bottles along the road. Invariably, Frankie would try to goad Todd into jumping off the bridge. He'd call him a chickenshit and a coward and then he'd climb up to the top rail and leap off himself. A couple of years ago, a boy from town had dived in headfirst and broke his neck. Todd imagined the snap of that stem every time Frankie hit the water. Once, after mixing beer and whiskey all morning, Frankie pressed his pistol to the back of Todd's head and ordered him to jump. "Go ahead and shoot, you sonofabitch," Todd said. "I'd be dead anyway." He could barely dog paddle, let alone high dive from forty feet. Getting his head blown off didn't scare him nearly as bad as the deep hole of water on the east side of the bridge. But after a minute or two, Frankie eased the hammer back and stuck the gun down in his pants. As he started to walk away, he said over his shoulder, "You can't be a pussy all your life, Todd. Someday you're just gonna have to say fuck it."

Once a month, Frankie would take off and spend the weekend with an old woman that lived over in Massieville. He'd lost all his confidence around pretty women after his face got mangled, but he told Todd he still needed to get a nut off once in a while. The hag didn't give a damn what he looked like, as long as he could make his hogleg stand up. On Sunday evenings, he'd come back to the fish camp bruised with denture marks and loaded down with food she'd packed for him: dusty jars of preserves, bread sacks of bloody turtle meat, sometimes a soggy pie. Todd would sniff the food and throw most of it out the door for the raccoons and possums. "I think she's trying to poison you," he said one day, peeling back the paper on a package of green hamburger.

"I got to find me something else," Frankie complained. "My God, she's awful. I might as well stick my dick in that jar of peaches."

"The way I figure it, something's always better than nothing," Todd said.

"Shit, how would you know?"

"Don't worry, I know." Todd went back to rummaging through the sack. He found a slab of macaroni and cheese wrapped up in tinfoil and set it off to the side.

"Well, let me ask you something then," Frankie said, looking down and picking at a brown scab on his arm. "How did you first figure out you was funny?"

Todd looked up, both surprised and alarmed by the question. "What the fuck's that mean? *Funny.*"

"I mean queer."

"Why do you want to know?" Todd said.

Frankie gave a little laugh. "Jesus, don't go getting any ideas. I'm just asking is all."

Todd thought for a moment. He'd rehearsed the story in

his head a thousand times, but nobody had ever asked him anything that personal before. "Remember that VISTA man a few years back?" he said, his voice suddenly shaky. In 1968, when Todd was fourteen, the government had sent a man named Gordon Biddle to Knockemstiff to help the hillbillies build a playground. He told everyone at the first meeting he held at the Shady Glen Church of Christ in Christian Union, "Better to work with the poor in America than fight the poor in Vietnam." Everyone in the pews, even the old men who had fought in World War Two, grinned and nodded at that, and before the night was over, they had accepted the outsider. For Todd, it had seemed as if everything about the VISTA man— his hair, his skin, even his glass eye—had glowed in the soft colored light coming through the cheap stained glass of the church. He had never met a man so beautiful, nor one so friendly. Within two weeks, he found himself high on weed and naked in the backseat of Gordon's beat-up Ford station wagon, and nearly every night after that for the rest of the summer. "Man, that seems like a long time ago," he said when he finished telling the story.

"You're shittin' me? So all that stuff was true?" Frankie said as he lit a cigarette. "That funny-talkin' fucker?"

"He was from New Jersey."

"That's some sick stuff, man."

"He didn't make me do nothing I didn't want to do," Todd said, though he didn't tell Frankie the whole story. Gordon had promised him that he'd take him away when he finished the ball diamond and headed back to New Jersey, and Todd was young enough to believe that he was telling the truth. All he had to do was keep quiet about the nights they spent in the back of the station wagon. But then a coon hunter saw them parked on Train Lane one night, and within a couple of days, ugly rumors about the VISTA man started cropping up all over Knockemstiff. By the time Todd heard the gossip, Gordon had already taken off. Things had gone downhill from there: a janitor in the broom closet at the high school, a few creepy perverts in the rest area over on Route 50. He laughed to himself; his love life was even worse than Frankenstein's.

Sometimes at night, they'd sit on opposite sides of the big room on old kitchen chairs that Frankie had salvaged from a dump over on Reub Hill. They would smoke and drink and pop whatever they'd been able to scrounge that day, and Frankie talked while Todd listened. By that time, Frankie's liver stuck out from his side like a baby's fist and often throbbed like a toothache. He'd sit and rub it like he was trying to coax a genie out of a bottle as he told his stories. Mostly they were about the Super Bee or some of the women he'd been with before the scar, but once in a while he recalled other crazy shit he had done. "Back four or five years ago," he said one night, "I ate a raw chicken, guts and all." For most of that week, they'd been smoking on a big block of mildewed Lebanese hash that a logger had sold them for practically nothing because it made people's gums bleed. The floor of the fish camp was sticky with bloody spit. Flies buzzed around them like they were dead meat.

"No way," Todd said. He had a finger jammed in his mouth, working a loose tooth back and forth. He couldn't leave it alone. He'd already lost one of his good ones since he'd started smoking the fungus.

"Goddamn I didn't," Frankie said. "Ask Bobby Shaffer, he'll tell you."

"Guts and everything? Fuck, man, that would have killed you."

Frankie didn't say anything, and Todd knew that something bad was coming. He reached up and touched his left eye, still tender from a sucker punch that had come out of nowhere the week before. Ever since he'd told the story about the VISTA man, it seemed as if things had turned to shit between them, and he suddenly realized that he no longer had any fantasies about Frankie and him making a life together. They had just been crazy ideas that he'd latched onto when he found himself all alone after his grandmother died. Most of the inheritance money was still in the jar. He could get out any time he wanted to.

In the dark room, Todd listened to Frankie take a couple swigs from a bottle of Wild Irish Rose he'd been nursing all evening. Something scurried across the floor, and he jerked his feet up. The silence grew, filled the dirty room. Musty-smelling hash fumes drifted out the doorway. A night bird called out from across the creek. "You callin' me a liar?" Frankie finally said, his voice barely a whisper.

Before Todd could answer, Frankie jumped up and knocked him off his chair onto the floor. His fists caught him seven or eight times in the side of the head, and Todd felt something bust in one of his ears. Then Frankie got his arm around Todd's neck and squeezed, shutting off his air. He kicked and tried to break loose and then felt nothing but a small black hole that fit around him like a sleeve. His last thought before he went under was that he would see his grandmother again. But after a while he woke up, lying on his belly on the bloody floor with his jeans down around his ankles. He rolled over and spit out his loose tooth. Frankie was standing over him, wiping his dick off with a rag. Raising his hips, Todd started to smile as he pulled his pants back up.

"What you grinnin' about, you little faggot?" Frankie said. Then he stomped down hard on Todd's face with the heel of his work boot.

When he finally woke up that second time, Frankie was gone, along with the Ford and the jar of money. All the rest of that night, Todd cried and kept apologizing to his grand-mother's ghost. It had taken her a lifetime to save that much money. When daylight came, he searched around and found two hits of blotter acid taped under the bottom of the hubcap they used as an ashtray and enough roaches to roll two skinny joints. Out back in a clump of weeds, he stumbled upon five bottles of beer in a paper sack. Frankie had taken most every-thing else, even the flashlight and Todd's little transistor radio.

Not knowing what else to do, he waited. He rationed his cigarettes, tried to sleep. His ear bled off and on. There were some canned blackberries in the cupboard left over from one of Frankie's visits to the old woman. They gave Todd the shits, but he ate them anyway. He rubbed the wall with a flat rock until the stick family disappeared. His forehead still had the boot print on it. Once he woke up thinking that his grand-mother was fixing him pancakes on top of the coal stove. By the end of the third day, he knew Frankie wasn't coming back.

That night, Todd ate the two hits of blotter and drank the last beer. Then he put on his shoes and walked through the weeds along the creek bank down to Schott's Bridge. It was three o'clock in the morning and traffic was dead. Everything was damp with dew. Todd walked back and forth across the smooth planks for a few minutes and then hoisted himself up onto the outer rail at one end of the bridge. It was slick. With his arms held out away from his body, he slowly made his way to the middle. Then he stopped and stared down into the black water for a long time, feeling the first tiny rushes of the acid streak through his brain. Todd lit his last cigarette and smoked it almost down to the filter. Then he let it drop, and the burning orange coal fell through the damp air. As he stood there, aching with sorrow and regret, he watched the water swallow it.

LARD

EVERYONE IN KNOCKEMSTIFF, OHIO, THOUGHT THAT DUANE Myers was going out with his first real woman that night, but he was just blowing smoke. He'd spread the rumor all over the holler, then covered the major details at the Torch Drive-in: smeared a glob of ketchup across the backseat of his father's Chrysler, spilled some wine on a pair of his sister's ragged panties, even branded two hickeys on his neck with a metal spoon that he heated up with a Zippo lighter. Then he spent the rest of the evening hunkered down behind the steering wheel like a toad, waiting to go home. He drank a six-pack of warm beer and watched *Women in Cages* and *Female Moonshiners*. The odor of scorched flesh lingered in the car like the smell of buttered popcorn.

Ever since Duane had turned sixteen that spring, his old man, Clarence, had been on his ass about finding a girlfriend. "What the hell's wrong with you?" the old man asked. "Goddamn, Duane, when I was your age, I was bustin' cherries all over this damn county." They were setting tomato plants out in the long, rocky garden that Clarence made the boy slave over every summer. The old man sucked down a beer for every three Big Boys that Duane stuck in the ground. Empty cans were scattered along the crooked rows like giant seed-pods. "I shit you not, boy," Clarence bragged, settling back on his skinny haunches and wiping sweat from his dirt-streaked brow, "one time I fucked a mud dauber's nest I was so god-damn horny." Duane kept moving forward silently on his knees, raking up lumpy clay mounds around each wilted plant with his hands. Clarence had been telling these stories forever; one day it was a bee's nest, then a sweaty sock, sometimes a pint of pig brains. It had always been a big joke, but things were different now.

By the middle of the summer, Clarence seemed to be on the verge of cracking up. He paced around the pasture behind the house sometimes for hours, stomping through cow shit and se-riously wondering if maybe his only son might be God's pun-ishment for a life that had been so littered with lust. At night he had nightmares that Duane was turning into a sissy like that Dixon boy from over on Plug Run, the one that got nabbed wearing his mother's nightgown, then moved to Columbus for a Swedish operation.

"You gotta quit readin' them books," Clarence warned Duane one morning at the kitchen table. He looked like hell, anyone could tell he'd had another fucked-up dream. "Start watchin' more TV," he advised. The old man took a sip of hot coffee, pushed away the plate of white bread and bologna gravy his sleepy wife had set in front of him.

Duane leaned against the door, gulping a glass of cold milk. His stomach had been on fire for weeks now. Trying to avoid his father's baggy, bloodshot eyes, he kept glancing nervously around the room until he finally caught his wavy reflection in a shiny copper skillet that hung on the wall. He stared at the purple craters sunk into his thin face, the black-framed glasses, the short choppy haircut that Clarence still insisted on. "Check out that Twiggy girl," he heard his father say. "By God, I'd take a piece of that."

The problem with Duane became the old man's favorite topic. He couldn't keep his mouth shut. Even the bastards that Clarence worked with at the paper mill got in on the act. Every day they waited until Clarence walked into the lunchroom, then started blowing off about finding dried jizz sparkling like doughnut glaze in the backseat of their junior's muscle car, used rubbers lying in the driveway like fat dead slugs. They kept feeding the old man new insults to throw at Duane: faggot, poofer, fudgepacker. It was like tossing logs on a fire. Clarence would come home wound tight as a clock, stomp through the kitchen door waving his sweaty, sawdust-covered arms, screaming "Pansy!" at the top of his lungs.

Duane's friends only made things worse. Just a couple of weeks after school started, Porter Watson and Wimpy Miller stopped by on their way to pull a train on Geraldine Stubbs. Clarence was standing in his socks under the walnut tree in the front yard drinking a quart of beer. As Duane climbed into the backseat of the Fairlane, Porter yelled, "Hey, Clarence, how's it going, man?"

"Shit," Duane muttered when he saw his father start ambling toward them.

"What you boys into tonight?" Clarence asked.

Porter grabbed a cigarette off the dash and stuck it between his lips. "Geraldine Stubbs," he answered with a grin.

Porter's black hair hung past his square shoulders as thick and shiny as any woman's. He wore cheap rings shaped like skulls and marijuana leaves that had turned his fingers a bluish-green color. He'd had more girls than you could shake a stick at. Earlier that summer, his mother had banished him to the garage after he brought home a dose of crabs and spread them all over her new couch.

"Who?" Clarence said, running a hand over his stiff, gray crew cut.

"One of them retards from over on Reub Hill," Wimpy spoke up, pulling a little black comb out of his mouth and running the spit through his thin red hair. Wimpy had a flat stupid face, long yellow teeth. He reminded Duane of a can opener.

"Nice?" the old man asked. He leaned against the car and tipped up the foamy beer.

Porter shrugged, took a drag on his cigarette, then said, "Well, she ain't much to look at, but she sure likes to spread 'em."

"Yeah," Wimpy cracked, "that's why they call her Peanut Butter."

Clarence slung the empty bottle in the grass. "How old?" he belched.

"Fifteen," Porter said.

Clarence pulled out a wrinkled pack of Red Man, dug out two fingers of chew, and shoved them in his mouth. He took a long look at the hills that surrounded the holler. The leaves were turning fast. Bright patches of red and orange stood out against the green pines. He hadn't had a hard-on in six months. "Hey, like I'm always tellin' Duane," he finally said in a solemn voice, "puss is puss. It's all good, just some better than other." He sounded like some ancient philosopher who'd

r the problem for centuries. Then he bent down
in at Duane, made wacky up-and-down signals
bushy eyebrows until Porter backed out of the driveway.

But Duane couldn't go through with it. They parked in
front of Geraldine's old house and leaned on the horn until
she finally came out. Stumbling through the weedy yard with
her head down, wrapped in her shabby clothes, she reminded
Duane of a timid ghost hovering just inches above the ground,
searching for an empty tomb to hide in. Then, to make matters worse, he had to sit beside her in the backseat all the way
to Train Lane while Wimpy argued with Porter about who
was going to get firsts. Geraldine never said a word, just sat
scrunched up against the door staring out the window, sucking down the beers Wimpy handed her. She smelled like pee,
had gray lint stuck in her frizzy brown hair.

"You're too damn picky," Porter said later, after they let
her out. "Fuck, your old man woulda tore that up." He jabbed
Wimpy in the arm and they both laughed.

"I ain't him," Duane said, staring down at the big wet spot
in the middle of the backseat.

Wimpy shook his head. "Yeah, Duane, what you wanta
do?" he said, lighting a joint. "End up like that crazy Lard and
his goddamn Cher?"

"Nancy," Duane corrected. Almost everyone made fun of
Lard McComis. Besides being the fattest kid in Knockemstiff,
he was crazy in love with Nancy Sinatra, the famous singer.
He knew everything about her, down to the size of her feet
and what kind of ice cream she liked to eat. But though Lard
was a couple bricks shy of a load, Duane still considered him
sharper than Wimpy any damn day.

"What?" Wimpy said.

"It ain't Cher, it's Nancy!" Duane yelled. Then he turned and watched Geraldine as she floated across the muddy ditch that ran alongside the gravel road and disappeared into the dark house. Nobody, he suddenly realized, had bothered to tell her good-bye or thanks or even see you next time, whore.

B Y THE TIME HE LEFT THE DRIVE-IN AND DROVE BACK TO Knockemstiff, Duane's beer buzz was gone along with his nerve. Topping the last steep hill before the holler, he slowed down, and then turned into Porter's rutted driveway. It was one o'clock in the morning, but a light still burned in the run-down garage. He dreaded facing the old man with a clear head tonight. Duane could picture Clarence sitting on the couch waiting up for him, a bottle cocked between his legs, anxious to examine evidence, ask dumb questions. Even talking to his old man on a good day felt like being trapped in an elevator with a cannibal who'd been off his feed.

Pulling in next to Porter's beat-up Ford, Duane shut off the engine and stuck his sister's wet panties in his pocket. He walked around the side of the building, pushed back the piece of heavy brown felt that served as a door, and looked in. Lard was sprawled out on two bales of musty straw, his greasy bibs pulled down around his scabby knees. A trouble lamp plugged into a frayed extension cord hung from one of the rafters above his head, shining down on his mountainous belly like a circus spotlight. A few feet away, Porter and Wimpy were passing a bong back and forth and tossing an occasional dart at the huge ball of fat. The darts were special ones with points that had been ground off until they were only an inch or so long. Every time one of the shafts found a sweet spot, the boys turned Lard on to another hit off the plastic pipe. It was the only sport they were any good at.

As soon as Duane stepped through the door, Lard grinned and yelled in his ducky voice, "Hey, Duane, see my girl-friend?" Then he held up his Nancy Sinatra album cover, the same one he'd shown Duane a million times before. It was her *Boots* LP, the one that transformed her from a spoiled rich brat into a bona fide sex goddess. She was all curled up like a cat in tight go-go shit, red leather skirt, knee-high boots. Lard car-ried it with him everywhere, stuck down the front of his bibs. Sometimes he used it as a shield, held it in front of his fat pasty face whenever someone got ready to chuck another bomber at him. He claimed he wanted to save his eyes.

Duane smiled and shook his head. "Damn, boy, ain't you got any other records?"

Lard whooped and hugged the record jacket, then planted a wet smacker on Nancy's frosted lips. "Not like her I don't, Duane," he said.

Porter tipped up a can of beer and killed it. "Man, am I glad you're here," he said to Duane. "You babysit the fat bas-tard for a while. He's gettin' to be a real pain in the ass."

"Aw, he's all right," Duane said. "Lardy, you been bad again?"

"No, Duane, it's him," Lard protested, pointing a stubby finger at Porter. "He drink too much Blue Ribbon."

Porter winked at Duane, then tossed his empty can at Lard's head. "Duane, them two's been at it like dogs all night," he said, yanking a cigarette lighter out of his pocket. "It ain't right. I say we light that cardboard bitch up unless the fat stud wants to start sharing."

"No! No!" Lard cried. He tried to stand up, but fell back

down. Pink sap ran slowly from a small puncture in his stomach, disappeared beneath the dunes of blubber. "Porter, you leave her alone," he wailed, rocking side to side on the straw bales.

Suddenly, out of the corner of his eye, Duane saw Wimpy cock his arm back. "Incoming!" Wimpy yelled. Duane watched Lard jerk the cardboard cover up to his face just as a dart bounced off his chest and stuck in the dirt floor. "Almost got you, you damn freak," Wimpy said.

"Darn you, Wimpy," Lard said, smearing the tears running down his cheeks with a dirty palm, "you put my eyes out, my granny gonna be mad."

"Okay, that's enough," Duane said. "Shit, you got him bleeding again."

"Hey, ain't nobody twistin' his arm," Porter said. "He asks for it."

It was true. Lard would do anything to get someone to pay attention to him. Sometimes late at night, after *Armchair Theater* signed off and the TV screen went dead, he would slip out of his granny's house and walk up and down the dark road that ran through Knockemstiff. He'd wake people up by tapping on their windows, then hold out his darts and plead with them to come out and toss a few. Then he'd step away from their house, unfasten his bibs and let them fall to the ground. His white belly shone as big and bright as the fucking moon. Listening to the mosquitoes buzz in his ears, he might stand there for hours, waiting for someone to walk out and try to throw a bull's-eye.

"Who cares?" Wimpy said. "Shit, his fuckin' gut's just one big scab anyway. That damn thing's hard as a turtle shell." He picked up a dart and started honing the short dull point against a grindstone lying on a workbench in the corner.

Duane handed Lard an oily rag that was lying on the floor. "Here, wipe yourself off. And fasten up those bibs."

Porter fired up the bong, passed it to Duane. "Fuck, man, what happened to your neck?"

Duane pushed his glasses up, felt his face begin to glow red with embarrassment. He'd never been a good liar. "She tried to eat me up," he answered. It was one of the lines he'd been rehearsing for his father.

Wimpy turned and squinted at Duane's neck. "Boy, I'd say. Look like she tried to chew yer whole damn head off."

Duane didn't reply, just wrapped his lips around the mouth of the bong and sucked up smoke through everybody's spit. The weed tasted vaguely of potato chips. In the light, he could see crumbs swirling in the bubbling water like tiny sea monkeys. He shuddered, then took another hit.

As soon as he had heard that Duane was taking a girl to the Torch Drive-in on Friday night, Porter had asked, "What's her name?" He and Wimpy were huddled around the work-bench in the garage, trying to wire an eight-track tape player to a leaky car battery.

Duane had spent weeks thinking up a name, went over a million of them in his head before finally stumbling across the perfect one. Already, he'd fallen in love with it, got hard every time it rolled off his tongue. "Mapel McAdams," he said slowly.

"She got any sisters?" Porter asked unexpectedly.

"Uh . . . no, she's an only kid," Duane answered, tipping up his RC Cola and chugging a long drink.

Wimpy looked up from the mess of wires he was wrapping

in black electrical tape. "I know her," he said out of the blue. Duane coughed and fizzy pop shot out his nose.

"What the hell?" Porter yelled, jumping back. He wiped RC off his face with a big hairy forearm. "Jesus, Duane."

Duane caught his breath. "Went down the wrong pipe," he sputtered. Then he turned to Wimpy. "How could you know her? She's a town girl."

"So?" Wimpy said. "My cousin Jimmy, he used to take her out." He leaned forward and bit the tape off, then added, "Yeah, he said she stunk so bad he had to roll the winders down."

"That creepy bastard's always talkin' shit," Duane said angrily. "This girl ain't no damn Geraldine." After all, they were talking about *Mapel McAdams*, not some zombie with dust balls in her hair. Besides, how could anyone know her? Duane wasn't even sure he'd recognize Mapel himself. Hell, he was still making her up.

"Well," Wimpy spat, "I bet you a dollar she's the same one."

"Aw, you stupid fuckin' . . ." Duane began, but then he shut up. It suddenly dawned on him that Wimpy's lie had just made his woman that much more believable. He looked up and stared for a moment at a mud dauber's nest plastered to one of the rafters. Then he walked away just as the tape deck shorted out in a shower of hot orange sparks.

"DUANE, YOU GONNA GET MARRIED NOW?" LARD ASKED. Duane was helping him pull up his bibs. A black fly was smashed flat below one of his sagging tits.

"No, Lardy, she's just some girl."

"More like a goddamn vampire," Porter said. "I hope you

didn't let her give you a blow job. From the looks of your neck, it'd be like stickin' your dick in a meat grinder."

Wimpy popped a beer, then asked, "So, Duane, what did it smell like? And don't lie either."

Duane paused to light his last cigarette, went over the prepared answer in his head once again. "Like a fish fry," he said.

"See, I told you, didn't I?" Wimpy said.

"Is she purty as Nancy?" Lard asked. He was looking down at the *Boots* record, tracing his finger over the pop singer's face.

"Jesus, you fat fuck," Wimpy said, "he just told us her snatch smelled like fish. What do you think, Duane's got himself a movie star?"

Porter stepped closer, peered at Duane's neck again. "So what did you end up doing with her?" he asked.

Duane sucked hard on his cigarette, tried to come off casual. "I soaked it in Boones Farm."

"Bullshit," Porter said. "Fucker, you won't even take a turn with old Geraldine."

Duane jerked the sticky panties from his pocket and held them up in the smoky air. "Oh, yeah?" he said. "Who you think these belong to?" He waved them in front of Porter's bloodshot eyes like a matador taunting a bull. They were the final piece of evidence. He could imagine his old man mounting the underwear to the living-room wall like a dead animal.

Porter grabbed his hand, held it tight while he cautiously sniffed the trophy. "You gotta be kiddin' me," he said. "You mean this Mapel girl, she actually let you do that?"

"Yeah," Duane swore, "she was into it. You can look. There's fuckin' apple wine all over the old man's car."

Porter turned to Wimpy. "Damn, maybe we oughta try

that shit on Geraldine," he said. "Douche it with wine before you start munchin' on it."

"Fuck you," Wimpy shot back.

"Better yet," Porter said, pointing across the garage, "rinse it with that goddamn gas can."

A

S SOON AS PORTER AND WIMPY PASSED OUT, LARD REACHED up and switched off the trouble lamp. "That light hurts my eyes," he muttered. Then he sank back down on the straw and stared quietly into the gloom. "Duane," he finally said, his voice now low and serious, "you shouldn't talk about your girlfriend that way."

Duane didn't say anything. He was stretched out in a wooden chair, smoking one of Porter's Camels, going over his story one more time before he went home to face the old man. A wave of disgust suddenly washed over him, soaking him in shame. Even though she wasn't real, he knew he'd treated Mapel badly, said stuff about her he wouldn't say about a dog. He whispered her name again, but it didn't feel the same now. She was gone. Taking another drag off the cigarette, he thought of Geraldine gliding across her yard after Porter and Wimpy were done with her.

They sat in silence for a few more minutes, then Lard spoke up again. "Duane?"

"What now?"

"Wanta trade?"

"Trade? Trade what?"

"I trade you my Nancy for your Mapel."

Duane looked over at Lard in surprise. The fat boy was clutching the Nancy album close to his heart, his huge stomach moving slowly up and down like a worn-out bellows. He'd had his Nancy for years now; they did everything together. She'd protected him from a thousand stray darts. "You don't want to do that, Lardy," Duane said.

"Why not?" Lard asked. He was still staring up into the rafters.

Duane thought for a minute. "Because . . . because she's your girl, always has been," he explained. "Heck, she's better than any ol' Mapel."

"Aw, Duane," Lard said with a yawn, "Nancy ain't even real. She's just some old picture my granny give me." Then he closed his eyes.

Duane waited a while, then stood up and pulled the damp panties out of his Levi jacket. He crept softly across the hard dirt floor and stood over his fat friend. Lard was snoring now, his flabby arms crossed over his belly. He smelled like potato chips and grimy sweat. Glancing over to make sure Porter and Wimpy were still asleep, Duane noticed the darts lined up in a row on the workbench. Ever since they were kids, Lard had claimed that he couldn't feel anything, insisted that the darts never hurt. Still, Duane had always pitched his underhanded, keeping a secret promise to himself never to break the fat boy's skin. "Like a goddamn girl," Wimpy liked to jeer.

Duane stuffed the panties into the side pocket of Lard's bibs, then gathered up all the darts and stepped outside into the night. He could hear the far-off rumble of a B&O freight as it rolled along the curved spine of the Summit heading west toward Cincinnati. Moving to the end of Porter's driveway, he stared down at his parents' house, moldering at the bottom of the hill like an illegal dump, surrounded by the old man's rusty junk and overgrown lilacs and gray October fog. He couldn't believe that he lived there.

As the sound of the train died away, the wind suddenly picked up, rattling the dry weeds in the field across the road.

The cool air tingled on his blistered neck. He saw his parents' porch light flash on, then off again. Looking up, he searched out the brightest star throbbing in the sky above Knockemstiff, then drew back and flung one of the darts at it. He kept throwing them, as hard as he could, until they had all disappeared into the darkness that surrounded him.

FISH STICKS

IT WAS THE DAY BEFORE HIS COUSIN'S FUNERAL AND DEL ended up at the Suds washing his black jeans at midnight. They were the only pants he owned that were fit for the occasion. Even Randy, the dead man who didn't give a fuck anymore, would look better than Del. The one decent shirt in his trash bag had TROY'S BAIT SHOP stenciled across the back of it.

That wasn't all. Del was with a woman he couldn't get rid of, no matter what he did or said. Every time he dumped her off at the group home, she beat him back to his room with a fresh load in her automatic pill dispenser and another wad of clean underwear. To make matters worse, she kept bugging the shit out of him with these fish sticks she reeled up from the bottomless pond of a plastic purse. They were cold and greasy, feathered with gray lint. And even though she was probably the best woman Del Murray had ever been with—gobs of bare-knuckle sex, the latest psychotropic drugs, a government check—he was still embarrassed to be seen with her in public.

Anyone who's ever dated a retard will understand what he was up against.

Del bought a box of soap from a little vending machine that charged exorbitant prices and poured most of it into the washer, then walked over to the bulletin board. Every Laundromat has one, a place on the wall where people can peddle their junk or swap their kids. There was a notice for a big tent revival over on the hopeless side of town, a crudely written flyer promising a better life, something that Del had craved for a long time. In one corner a cartoon Jesus floated on a pink cloud above the earth, in the other a bloody fiend sat in a prison cell snacking on a plate of skulls labeled like homemade preserves: JUNKIE, WINO, HOMO, WHORE, ATHEIST. It was designed to scare the fuck out of the type of people who wash their clothes in a public place. But more than anything, the poster dredged up memories for Del, reminded him of the time he and Randy wasted an entire year attending the Shady Glen Church of Christ in Christian Union just to win a prize, a little red Bible that fell apart the first hot day. They were eight years old.

SEVERAL YEARS AFTER THEY DROPPED OUT OF SUNDAY school, Randy and Del enrolled in a mail order Charles Atlas course. This was back in the days when a kid could still change the course of his life by filling out one of the order forms found in the back of a comic book, a long time ago, years before the Fish Stick Girl was even born. A new envelope filled with exercises arrived in the mail every week, but Del couldn't get into it, all that work just so you could tear a phone book in half. Instead, he shoplifted a paperback from Gray's Drugstore in Meade called *"Reds."* Del wasn't much of a reader, but he needed something to kill time until Randy gave up on building a different body.

Del would never forget *"Reds."* He probably read it a dozen times that summer. It had the same powerful effect on him as the public service announcement on the radio about the guy who ripped his arm open with a can opener so he could blow dope in the bloody hole with a plastic straw. In the book, a clean-cut hero named Cole picks up these two runaway girls who shoot sleeping pills in his dad's new Lincoln. For Del, it was like flipping on a light switch, and by the time the crazy bitches dropped acid and torched the hippie's crash pad, he knew exactly how he wanted to live his life.

"Man, you gotta read this," Del said, waving his copy of *"Reds"* under Randy's nose. They were listening to a Hendrix album while Randy stood in front of the open window and worked out in the nude. Charles Atlas was big on sunshine and fresh air, which probably would have been fine if you lived on the moon, but in their county, the smog from the paper mill made everything smell like rotten eggs. Randy had already scratched the shit out of "Purple Haze," and Jimi kept repeating ". . . while I kiss the sky . . . while I kiss the sky." Glancing out the window over Randy's shoulder, Del saw a dirty brown cloud drifting by, high over Knockemstiff, the holler where they lived.

Randy glanced at the cover of the book, the picture of the four-eyed boy and the two wasted chicks standing by a highway sign with their thumbs in their pockets. He snorted in disgust, then took a big gulp from the jelly glass of raw eggs he kept by the bed. He was up to a dozen a day. Sweat was dripping off the end of his dick. His stomach resembled a car grill. "I could break that sonofabitch like a pencil," he said, flexing his biceps.

"Shoot, this guy gets more pussy than you ever dreamed of," Del said. "He don't need no muscles either."

"Bullshit. Girls love muscles. What about the guy who gets sand kicked in his face down at the beach?" Randy asked.

"You don't even like to swim," Del pointed out. "Look, girls don't care how many push-ups you can do. They just want to get high and wear flowers in their hair. Maybe steal a car."

"Yeah, then we end up in jail like your brothers."

"Hey, I begged them to read this before they broke into that gas station," Del said.

"What the hell are you talking about?" Randy yelled. He'd already started another set of leg lifts. Del reached over and cranked up "I Don't Live Today" past the little piece of tape that Randy's brother, Albert, had stuck on the volume control. The speakers started making a funny noise, like someone was pounding the piss out of them with one of the dumbbells lying on the floor.

"I say we go to Florida and find these girls," Del said, holding the cover up to Randy's red, pimply face. "It's like hippie heaven down there."

"Damn, Delbert, that little one looks like somebody's sister," Randy grunted, just before the speakers blew.

THE FISH STICK GIRL TOOK OFF HER ARMY JACKET AND loosened the belt on her shiny jeans, then got down on the floor in the Laundromat amid the fuzz balls and cigarette butts and started doing stretches. Del figured that somewhere along the way, probably the night he hogged all of her Haldol, he'd confessed that he got a kick out of watching other people work out. It wasn't a kinky sex thing, but more like the pleasure a person gets out of seeing their best friend lose a job or some rich bastard go down in a plane crash. He wondered what other secrets he might have revealed. Del watched his pants slosh around in the window and tried to ignore the sexy sighs the Fish Stick Girl emitted with each slow movement. Though she'd been cursed with certain defects, she could bend into shapes that most people associate only with circus freaks and world-class contortionists. It was, he knew, just another part of her plan to make him a slave.

ON THE BUS GOING TO FLORIDA, DEL READ RANDY THE juiciest passages in *"Reds"* over and over, but always avoided the ending. By the time they hit Atlanta, Randy had even memorized the entire chapter about the Spanish fly orgy in the abandoned beach house. He became convinced that the psychotic Dorcie would be waiting for him when they pulled into the station at St. Petersburg. After his cousin nodded off, Del slipped back to the restroom and tore out the last few pages of the novel. He didn't have the heart to tell Randy that Dorcie, his little needle queen, had jumped off a bridge and drowned when the cops started closing in.

"I'M HUNGRY, MAN," RANDY SAID, THE MORNING THEY HIT the Florida state line. There were rows of orange trees along the highway. Everything smelled like air freshener.

"Look, those oranges are big as basketballs."

"No, I mean I'm losing muscle fast," Randy said. "I got to find some eggs." It was true—Randy was starting to look like a rubber doll that had stepped on a nail. He was deflating before Del's eyes.

"We'll buy a dozen as soon as we get some money."

"How we do that?" Randy asked, his voice cracking. "Does it say in that book how we do that?"

"Don't worry," Del said. "This guy tells you everything."

THREE DAYS LATER IN ST. PETERSBURG, THEY MET A HOT-dog vendor named Leo. He was dumping new meat into a stainless-steel steamer. The smell of snouts and eyeballs wafting from the stand had been driving Del and Randy crazy ever since they'd started sleeping under the pier. "Come by my place this evening, you," Leo said, handing the boys a couple of dogs along with an address scrawled on a matchbook. "Go ahead, eat up, you," he said, winking at Randy.

"Hey, Del," Randy said later, "you think that guy's funny?" Dried mustard was plastered on his chin.

"Who cares? I can't go home, that's all I know. My mom will kill me."

"How much you figure people will pay for something like that?" Randy said.

LEO CAME TO THE DOOR WEARING A FLOWERED BATHROBE and a pair of old tennis shoes with the toes cut out of them. His swollen feet looked like a pair of sea urchins. He lived in a sad motel room, with black tar footprints on the dirty carpet, somebody else's sand in the tub. It was the kind of place that Del would always gravitate toward later on, the kind of dump where something always happens that nobody wants to admit happened.

"He can wait outside," Leo said, nodding over at Del.

"No way," Randy said. "I ain't staying here by myself."

"What? You think I'm going to bite it off? Nibble it like a little fish stick?" Leo said, laughing. "All right. At least have him stand over in the corner so I don't have to look at him, you little fraidy cat, you." Then he handed Randy an old wrinkled *Playboy* to look at while he got ready. The magazine was evidently Leo's idea of foreplay, but some other kid had already drawn pointy beards on all the naked women.

While Leo was in the bathroom gargling mouthwash, Randy instructed Del to smack the bastard in the head if he saw any blood. "You heard what he said," Randy whispered. "Shit, he might be a cannibal for all we know." He pointed at a lamp by the bed that had blue seagulls flying around a yellow shade. He grabbed Del by the shoulders. "Don't fuck this up," Randy said. Del walked over and pulled the lamp plug out of the wall. Then he stepped into the corner and listened to the ocean just a block away. He could hear little kids squealing in the undertow, happy vacationers laughing in the sand. The whole world seemed louder that day at the Sea Breeze Motel.

"WHAT YOU THINKING?" THE FISH STICK GIRL ASKED. She'd finished her workout and was washing her hair in one of the big metal tubs with the last of Del's detergent. She wore her hair parted down the middle, one side dyed jet-black and the other side platinum blonde. It made her look like she had two heads.

"Nothing," Del said, staring out the window at the SUDS sign swaying gently back and forth in the wind.

"Jeez, what an answer," she said. "You always say the same thing."

"Well, don't ask then." Somebody had etched WILL WORK FOR DOPE across the grime of the window with a shaky finger. Del turned away satisfied that he would never get *that* bad.

The Fish Stick Girl turned off the spigot and began squeezing the soapy water out of her hair. "Sweetie, I'm telling you," she said, "your best bet is the Henry J. Hamilton Rehabilitation Center. It's a lot of paperwork, but I know some people."

"What makes you say shit like that?" Del asked. He lit a cigarette, ignoring the NO SMOKING signs hanging everywhere.

"Because you're the type that does well in a constructive environment," she explained, sounding like she was reciting a poem. "I noticed that the first time I saw you. At least you should take the test."

Del decided to ignore her. "I keep thinking about the time Randy and me went to Florida. I ain't never been that hungry. You couldn't buy a job, it was so bad."

"You used to work?" she asked incredulously.

"Well, it was a different world back then."

"I got more fish sticks," she said, reaching for her big purse.

"Put those goddamn things away," Del said. "It was almost thirty years ago."

"You never go hungry at the Henry J. Hamilton Center," she said. "They have special activities. Wanda keeps track of your SSI. Shoot, they even have some old lady do your laundry. We could be snuggled up watching TV right now. I always tip her a fish stick."

"Look, I told you, I ain't moving in that place!" Del yelled.

"Suit yourself. So why did you go to Florida?"

"I don't know," Del said. "I read this book. I guess you could say we were looking for a better life."

"Did you find it?" the Fish Stick Girl asked.

"No, it was just a goddamn book. I ain't read one since."

W HEN LEO FINISHED WITH RANDY, HE MOTIONED FOR DEL to help him up. The old man was gasping for air. Del could hear his knees crackle as he stood up. They sounded like a landslide in an old cowboy movie. A white dab of Randy's jizz lay on his bottom lip like a salted slug. Leo's bathrobe came loose, revealing purple stretch marks that crisscrossed

his bloated belly. Then he farted and limped over to his Lister-
ine bottle, tipped it up like a wino with a jug. Randy just stood
there like a gas station loafer, silent and dazed, waiting for another car to pull in.

Leo scooped some change out of a jar and sprinkled it in
Randy's hand like he was pouring gold dust into a little bag.
"That's it?" Randy finally said, staring down at the nickels,
dimes, and quarters.

"There's quite a bit of money there," Leo said.

"I let you suck my dick!" Randy yelled.

"Quiet down, you," Leo ordered. "That's all I'll pay for
something like that. You got a lot to learn, you. I could have
had more fun with a slab of bacon." He pulled a sweet roll
from the pocket of his robe and chomped the end off it.
"Now," he said, "take your ugly friend and get out of here,
you. Boys like you are nothing but trouble." Flaky crumbs
floated through the air like tiny golden gnats.

Randy looked over at Del and nodded. "I want more," he
said, and Del swung the lamp at the fat man's head.

THE FISH STICK GIRL GRABBED HOLD OF ONE OF THE METAL
poles that people hang their clothes on and started
twirling like a dancer in a strip club. Del dropped his soggy
jeans in the dryer and walked back over to the window. He
watched her reflection spin faster and faster in the glass. Her
long hair flew behind her like a cape. It seemed to Del that she
would surely fly into the wall or bounce off one of the big
metal machines. She began emitting a high-pitched squeal
that sounded like an ambulance rushing down the highway
looking for something to feed upon. Del backed away and
waited for the inevitable crash. It was like being at the Atomic

Speedway on family night, hoping for someone to fuck up and die so the kids would have a good time.

NOT LONG AFTER RANDY WON THE MR. OHIO CONTEST, DEL stopped by to ask a favor. "No way," Randy said. "You never pay back." He was leaned back in a chair behind a gray metal desk in the garage he ran with his brother, Albert. The big trophy sat behind him on a shelf.

"You're famous now," Del said, figuring he'd try a new angle. "What's that feel like?"

"Hell, I don't know," Randy said. "It don't make me no money if that's what you mean. I didn't even get the Bob Evans commercial." He kept squeezing a little rubber ball with his hand. His ears flexed every time he mashed it. Del couldn't imagine him selling sausage patties on TV.

"Look, man, I ain't never said anything about what happened in Florida, you know that."

"Ha! Delbert, that's all you ever talk about," Randy said. "Shit, you even told Sheriff Matthews."

"How about two hundred?" Del asked. "They won't let me back in my room."

"I ain't got it. You realize how much the drugs cost to win a big contest? I got more tied up in these arms than you'll steal in your lifetime," Randy said. "Look, I'm not telling you what to do, but you better get out of here before Albert comes back. He ain't liked you since you fucked up his stereo that time."

EVENTUALLY RANDY'S HEART GREW TOO BIG FOR HIS BODY. He was one of those pincushions who never take a break, the kind that get hooked on size regardless of the consequences. "They won't let me smoke," he wheezed when Del stopped by the rest home to see him. Del looked over at the oxygen tank standing beside the hospital bed. The nurse had told Del that Randy was strapped down because the medication made him hallucinate. He hoped maybe his cousin had some pills stashed away.

"Shit, you don't smoke," Del said. "What would Mr. Charles Atlas say about that?"

"I'm way beyond old Chuck now," Randy said. "Give me a weed."

"Maybe they just want you to get better," Del said weakly.

"Fuck that, I'm a dead man. They say my ticker's big as a football. C'mon, Delbert, gimme a fuckin' cigarette." Del loosened the top restraints, and handed Randy his pack. "Watch that door," Randy said. "That one aide is a real bitch."

Del watched Randy gag on the cigarette in between hits off the oxygen mask. "Hey," Del finally said, "remember that book I used to read all the time? Dorcie and Cole and . . . shit, I can't remember the other one."

"Holly," Randy said. "Her name was Holly. She was practically a virgin."

"Yeah, that's right. Jesus, I can't believe you remember her name."

"Now that Dorcie was something else," Randy said. "God, I wish I'd met her when I was benching six hundred. I'd have tore that up."

"Christ, Randy, it was just a book. I mean, those people weren't real or anything."

"Oh, no, you're wrong, man," Randy said. "They was real. More real than most shit anyway. I still think about her. What's that tell you?"

"What about the old man then?" Del whispered, leaning in close to the bed. "Do you still think about him?"

"Jesus, Delbert, you act like that's the only thing in your life that ever really happened. Fuck that old bastard. He got what he deserved, the way I see it." Del stood up and began pacing around the room. "Hey, while you're up, hand me that magazine there," Randy said. Del glanced around, saw an old copy of *Ohio Bodybuilder* on the windowsill. There was a picture of Randy on the cover. Del looked at his cousin in the faded photo, the victory smile, veins popping out everywhere. He handed over the magazine just as Randy took another hit off the cigarette and started coughing. It sounded as if someone was busting his chest apart with a jackhammer. He dropped the cigarette on the bed next to the oxygen mask. A small fire erupted in the sheets. When Del grabbed the water pitcher, Randy waved him away. "Get the fuck out of here," he gasped. As Del hurried out the door, he turned back to see Randy ripping up the magazine and feeding photos of his glory days to the flames.

DEL HAD THE FEELING THAT HE'D GO ON FOREVER, WHICH is a great feeling really, especially after you've watched your cousin commit suicide with a Marlboro. When the Fish Stick Girl finished her acrobatics and slid down the pole out of breath, he pushed her down on her knees behind the restroom door. "Act like you're doing this for money," he said urgently, unzipping his pants.

"Here?"

"Why not?" Del said. "This place is dead tonight."

"How much money?" she asked, settling back on her heels.

"I don't know. Enough to buy a hot dog."

"A hot dog?"

"Not much, just some change," Del answered, placing his hands on her wet hair. He closed his eyes and began to hear the ocean off the Florida coast in the dryer's muffled rumblings. Inhaling the dank laundry smells, he thought of Leo's mildewed carpet. He pictured the lamp in his sweaty hands, felt the weight of it, saw the seagulls make another pass around the shade. The Fish Stick Girl kept banging her face into his groin, and for a moment Del was fifteen again. He was on a Greyhound going south and reading that section in *"Reds"* where Dorcie fires up barbiturates for the first time. Randy was sitting beside him squeezing his pecs together and urging him to jump ahead to the chapter about the black guy named King Coon who knocked the white girls up with his thumb. Then they were laughing, pointing their own thumbs at some blond woman seated across the aisle. When Del realized it was over, he looked down and saw the Fish Stick Girl smiling up at him. He'd forgotten all about her.

After he folded his clean black jeans, Del and the Fish Stick Girl left the Suds and headed up the street. It was one o'clock in the morning and the air was cool and damp with dew. "Boy, you sure get into it," the Fish Stick Girl said. "What was so funny?"

"I think I saw my cousin."

"Nobody ever told me that before," she said. "Have you been taking my meds again?"

"Well, I appreciate it anyway," he said.

"You're welcome. Now you do something for me," she said, opening up her purse.

"What's that?"

"Here," she said, shoving a fish stick in Del's face.

Del hesitated, then grabbed the fish stick and bit a cold chunk off one end. It didn't taste like fish at all, but he imagined it was something else anyway, the way the devout do with the little wafer and the grape juice. "Okay, now close your eyes," she said. Del shut his eyes. "Don't peek," she ordered. As she pulled him down the street, he pretended not to know where they were going. She liked that. Cracking his eyes open, Del saw thick black clouds move across the sky and cover the moon like a grave blanket. He closed his eyes again and crammed the rest of the fish stick into his mouth. Suddenly, he was very tired. He felt like the ragged ghoul staggering across the screen in an old movie, the peace he sought always out of reach. They walked on, the Fish Stick Girl leading him by the hand.

BACTINE

I'D BEEN STAYING OUT AROUND MASSIEVILLE WITH MY CRIP-
pled uncle because I was broke and unwanted everywhere
else, and I spent most of my days changing his slop bucket and
sticking fresh cigarettes in his smoke hole. Every twenty-four
hours, I wiped him off with a wet cloth and turned his broken
body over to air everything out. He'd been totaled in a freak
car crash and had ended up with a giant settlement that cursed
him with enough money to vegetate for the rest of his sorry-
ass life.

I was supposed to be staying straight—his daughter had
even insisted I sign a goddamn scrap of paper—but late one
night I found myself fucked up in a strange car littered with
flakes of dead skin and stolen tools and those gas station cassettes that are always on sale for $1.99. The driver was a hill-
billy guy named Jimmy who kept calling me cousin, but I
couldn't even remember meeting him—let alone seeing him at
one of the reunions we used to have when our family was still
permitted in the state parks. Still, being the type of person I

was, I'd apparently let him talk me into huffing several cans of Bactine, and then I was sick, and my brain felt like a frozen bleach bottle. As snow swirled all around us in the Wal-Mart parking lot, I rinsed the inside of my face with Jimmy's last beer and vowed never to stick my head in a bread sack again.

Some time after that, around 3:00 AM, we ended up at the Crispie Creme looking for Phil, a friend of mine, who was supposed to have some Seconal suppositories left over from his dead dad's unsuccessful bout with cancer. The Creme is the only thing open in our town after the bars close where you might find people like us, but there was just Mrs. Leach, the cross-eyed waitress who always creeped me out because once, in jail, I'd held her son in my arms. Wherever I went in those days, I stumbled across the bill collectors and misfortunes of my past, while any chance of a future worth living kept spinning farther and farther away.

We ordered coffee, and then Jimmy and I sat down in a corner booth away from the old lady so she didn't have to look at us. Why worry an old woman at that time of night? The place was all windows and plastic woodwork and those buzzing fluorescent lights that always make me look like a corpse. A radio in the back was playing a fast Christmas song that only religious people could understand.

"That's the last time I do any of that stuff," I said. "I was talkin' to fucking Fred Flintstone that last can." Fumbling with a cigarette, I took a chance, surprised I didn't ignite from all the fumes I'd inhaled.

"Fuck, all I ever get is the sirens and those goddamn goofy lights." Jimmy pushed back a wad of crusty hair. He had sideburns that didn't match, and the eyes of a man you wouldn't trust with a milk cow. "One time though, out at the Torch Drive-in, I did get eaten by a giant bird." He said this with great feeling, like he was recalling his first kiss or the best day he ever lived. "Sonofabitch pulled me up outta the car like I was a little worm. Damn, cousin, that was a good time."

Mrs. Leach brought the pot, set down two cups smeared with orange lipstick and chocolate thumbprints. Looking up at her, Jimmy asked, "Hey, girl, how's that ol' Lester doing these days?" I motioned with my hand for him to shut up, but he'd already blurted it out.

"Cream?" was all she said. Though she was looking at Jimmy, her face was turned toward me because of the awful way her eyes were scrambled. Heartache and ridicule and the night shift had turned her into a coffee-spilling zombie. You could have nailed a cross to her forehead and the woman wouldn't have changed her expression. Then, without waiting for a reply, she turned and trudged back to the shiny counter, her white waitress pants saggy in the ass and stained with coffee spots and doughnut grease. If I were a man running for office, she was just the kind of person I might appeal to.

"What the fuck's the matter with you? Don't you know he's dead?" I said in a low voice, hoping the mom wouldn't hear.

"Who died?" Jimmy asked, tearing open a little plastic thimble full of artificial cream. "You mean Lester?"

"He's the one hung himself in the jail last summer," I whispered, covering my cup with my hand as some of the red, crusty skin around his mouth flaked off and dropped onto the table.

"Shit," Jimmy said loudly, slapping his tattooed hands together, "I remember now." He lit a cigarette, then glanced back at Lester's mom. She was picking pieces of lint off her frayed sweater, dropping them to the floor like little mashed cooties. "Oh, well," he said, shrugging his skinny shoulders, "what you gonna do? Hell, me and Lester went to school together." He motioned with his cup toward Mrs. Leach. "I knowed that old bag all my life."

Then, without thinking, I said, "I was there when they cut him down." It seemed that I always talked about shit that I didn't want to talk about, but could never say the things I wanted to say. "Had a trash bag wrapped around his neck," I added. I could still see the young deputy, dropping his big key ring, screaming on the radio for backup. Before I knew it, I'd wrapped my arms around Lester's quivering legs and lifted him up, his piss soaking through the top of my orange jumpsuit. I was doing ten shamefaced days for shoplifting a lousy package of cheese, and for a brief second or two, I saw saving him as a chance to prove that I was better than that. But when the deputy ran down the stairs, I grew confused, then limp. I hoped nobody would know the difference. The day before, Lester had pushed a pencil up his dick. It was his greatest accomplishment. I'll never forget the way he kicked when I let him go.

"I can see killin' yourself, but not with no fucking trash bag," Jimmy said.

"You keep doing that spray lube and shit, you won't have to worry about it."

The glass door swung open and two big, homely women walked in looking guilty. They were the kind of women who, out of sheer loneliness, end up doing kinky stuff with candy bars, wake up with apple fritters in their hair. They looked over at us with bold little smiles that indicated either stupidity or desperation. Jimmy leaned back in the booth, eyeing them like a desert sheikh buying a keeper at a white-slave auction.

"Well, well, well," he said.

"No way," I told him.

"Shit, I ain't had none in a month. I'd blow the top of that one's head off."

The older woman waddled over and squeezed into a booth opposite the counter while the young one stood and ordered a big box of day-olds and two quarts of hot chocolate. She was packed in a pair of those stretch pants that overweight people should be thrown in prison for wearing. A faded Reds ball cap was cocked on her head at an angle that seemed to foretell, in my gloomy state, an ill-fated ride with a stranger. I could almost see a garden of moss slowly spreading over her secret resting place.

"Want me to talk to 'em?" Jimmy offered, between attempts to attract the younger one by extending his tongue until it touched the tip of his runny nose.

"Nah, they're here for the sweets," I said. "Besides, I ain't never screwed a big woman and ain't about to start now."

"What the hell? Fat girls like to fuck, too. I can't believe someone like you is so goddamn picky."

"Why's that?" I asked, setting down my coffee cup.

"Well, your teeth and all. You'd be doing good to screw that old girl. You ain't exactly Glen Campbell."

I'd had enough of his mouth. Grabbing hold of his collar, I jerked him across the table. "You little sonofabitch," I said, twisting the dirty shirt around his skinny neck, "you just don't know when to shut up, do you?"

I choked him until his tongue popped out, then shoved him back down in the booth. He coughed and spit a gob of thick poisonous snot out onto the worn linoleum. "Jesus, man, I didn't mean nothing," he said, rubbing his throat.

"Just mind your own business, okay?" I said. Turning away, I looked out the window at the snowy street, hoping someone would show up with enough stuff to put me under. At one time, I'd practically been considered a handsome man, a regular party boy; decent women called me by my real name while the strippers at Tater Brown's let me light their cigarettes. But that was before some ugly bastard named Tex Colburn caught me in the Paint Creek bottoms picking through a patch of buds that he'd been planning on ripping off himself. By the time he ran me down in that cornfield, he was so pissed that he had his boys hold me while he chipped my front teeth out one by one with a spike nail he pulled out of a rotten fence post. Every time I flinched, he cut up my lips. Now I was at the mercy of a welfare dentist who spent his office hours at the clinic trading spit with the volunteer eye doctor. In the reflection from the glass, I tried out one of my old smiles. But the happy-shit days were gone, and I sat staring somberly into a pink, toothless cave.

"Well, fuck," I said after a few minutes, and turned back to face Jimmy, who was busy pouring sugar out of the dispenser and dividing it into two lines with a coffee spoon. "What you think?"

"Hey, I don't even know this Phil fucker," he said. "We just gonna sit around all night, or what?"

A clock shaped like a doughnut said 4:20 AM. Though I hated to admit it, Phil was probably passed out somewhere, enjoying his dead father's legacy. I found myself wishing I had a loved one who would die and leave me their barbiturates, but I couldn't think of anyone who'd ever loved me that much. My uncle had already promised his to the mail lady.

"Goddamn him," I said, half expecting Jimmy to snort the white crystals spread out on the table.

"We could always do another can," he suggested, his face hovering just inches above the glittering columns.

I thought about going back to my uncle's house, snaking out the clogged tubes, listening to the poor bastard repeat the same bitter stories over and over again. Behind us, the two big women were busy exchanging obscene fantasies, making suction sounds with their mouths, while poor Mrs. Leach dozed on her blue feet behind the display case. "Man, that shit just eats me up," I groaned, already feeling pukey from the thought of the ether smell.

Detecting a hint of surrender in my voice, Jimmy looked up and smiled with all his soft, twisted teeth. "You just say the word, cuz," he told me.

I decided to ignore him. Besides, what was there to say? Because of who we were, I already knew what we would do. In a few minutes, Jimmy and I would leave this place and go find somewhere to park in his filthy car. He would fill up the plastic bag again with Bactine, and I would sit and listen to him suck the cold fog down into his lungs. The smell of it would sicken me, and I would crack the window. The snow would slowly cover the windshield. Jimmy's eyes would turn as red and sticky as candy, and his head would fall back against the seat in a dream. If he were lucky tonight, maybe he would see something that he hadn't seen before. And then it would be my turn.

DISCIPLINE

WE DROVE DOWN TO PARKERSBURG TO COP SOME MORE 'roids—fifty ccs of Mexican Deca for 425 American dollars—and I fixed up my son, Sammy, right there in the parking lot of the Gold's, one cc in the hip. Deca is thick as molasses, tough shit to inject, but it won't bloat you up like a fucking Amish ham, either. He started whimpering like a little girl even before I found the sweet spot. "Stay focused," I said, pushing the plunger down slowly with my thumb. "Remember: Mr. South Ohio. No pain, no fucking gain." Sammy's dumb, zit-faced cousin Little Ralph was with us, hanging over the front seat, saying, "Let me do it, let me do it," until I had to slap the mouth right off him. Then I stuck my *Best of Sousa* tape in the stereo and lit up a serious fattie for the long haul back. I could listen to "The Gladiator March" all fucking day long. It's the music I used to play with my routine when I was competing.

Nobody said another word, except for Little Ralph as he spat blood out the back window, until we swooped off the exit ramp on the other side of town and damn near collided with a clusterfuck in front of the McDonald's. For a second, I thought I'd taken a wrong turn somewhere. I mean, it was the first traffic jam I'd ever seen in Meade, Ohio. Then I figured it had to be a fire, or maybe some drunken sonofabitch had crashed his car pulling out of the Tecumseh Lounge. But that wasn't it at all.

Bobby Lowe was standing out along the main drag doing a double bicep. It was the middle of December, definitely sweatshirt weather, but all he had on was a pair of radiant white briefs. I'd heard he'd been hitting the juice, but I had no idea how much size he'd gained. His arms were nearly as big as mine. Cars and trucks were lined up along Main Street, people honking their horns and whooping every time he hit a new pose, the way the trashy bastards show their appreciation around here. Bobby was mostly running through the seven classics, shit any retard can do. He was staring straight ahead, the sweat glistening on him even in the cold, shaking like a dog shitting razor blades. Nobody realizes how hard it is to hold a pose for ninety seconds and squeeze a year's worth of your life into it. Imagine some sonofabitch holding a gun to your head and forcing you to eat shit forever, like in hell.

"Fuck, why didn't we think of that?" Little Ralph said as two babes ran up and put hickeys on Bobby's biceps, then skipped back to their Mustang. That even made me hard, watching the one little bitch in the hip-huggers suck on his cannons.

"What would a fat fuck like you do out there?" I said to Ralph as I eyeballed Bobby's calves. The bastards must have been a good nineteen inches.

"Maybe get some face for one thing," he cracked.

"I'd hate to see the dirty skank that would go down on you," I shot back. "Shit, she'd turn the whole fuckin' town to stone."

"You oughta know," Sammy said, a goddamn smirk stretched across his face.

"Watch yourself, boy," I said. "Besides, that ain't a bit professional. He might as well be prancing around in some strip show." I still couldn't get over the size of Bobby's arms, which probably had a good two inches on Sammy's. And then, with a sickening feeling, I suddenly realized that Willard Lowe's son was going to beat Sammy for the South Ohio, him of all the people in the goddamn state. Willard Lowe was my one true enemy; I'd hated that prick since we used to fight over the plastic weight set in fourth-grade gym class.

"Aw, Luther, I'm just talkin' for fun," Little Ralph said.

"Hey, go ahead, Ralphie," I said. "Get on over there and shake your flabby ass for those fucking drunks."

"I didn't mean—"

"You fuckin' faggots are all the same, no discipline at all," I said. "Don't talk that shit no more. He's just showing off like some little punk in school." As soon as I said that, Willard Lowe walked out of McDonald's with a cup of coffee. He had that big grin on his face that shows off all his perfect white teeth: the same one he used to taunt me with back in the old days whenever we went up against each other. Nobody realizes how important the smile is in a contest. I'd be the first to admit, I never could smile worth a shit; people always said I looked like a starving rat clamping down on a chicken neck. It was my only defect, but it cost me the Midwest title seven years in a row. Still, Willard's lost his juice now, gave up pumping iron for big buckets of slop and an old lady's treadmill, so I guess, in the end, I won after all. He's just another lazy bastard now and the world's full of *them*.

We drove on back to the Power House; I mixed Sammy up some protein, then ordered him to hit the sack. I had the only true weight gym in southern Ohio, no women, no aerobics, no Nautilus shit. But since it was damn near impossible to find any decent bodybuilders around here, I had to rely on fat-ass powerlifters or the occasional football player to keep the place open. It used to be a gas station, and Sammy and I slept in the back. On rainy nights the fumes rising out of the oil-stained cement smelled like dinosaur blood.

A couple of days after Bobby Lowe made an ass out of himself in front of the McDonald's, he stopped over at the gym. I knew immediately something was up; his old man used to pull the same kind of shit right before a contest. "I thought it up myself," he started explaining. "Extreme posing, that's what I call it. The more fucked the situation, the better. Shit, I even got ESPN willing to come down and take a look. We're talkin' big money here, Luther."

"So?" I said.

"Well, I thought I could get Sam over there next Saturday. Make it a little contest. The other night was just a trial run."

"Get the fuck out of here," I said. "Sammy's training for the South Ohio."

"Hey, Dad," Sammy said, "I think—"

"Shut up!" I yelled and then turned back to Bobby. "Look, I know what you're doing. Your old man was the same way, always fucking with me. Him and that goddamn stupid grin of his. Now get the fuck out of my gym!"

"Gym?" he said, glancing around. "More like a fuckin'

prison maybe." Then he turned and strutted out like hot shit, his lats scraping the paint off the doorframe.

I cranked up the discipline that week, three sessions a day. Sammy was too gutted at night to even untie his lifting shoes, just slept propped up in the corner like a bag of shit. But it was the only way we were going to win; he'd taken after his skinny-ass mother, just a little bird of a thing who kept sneaking cigarettes and coffee until the cancer got her. I kicked myself a thousand times for not knocking up some fat-ass Amazon with big bones. Still, with the Deca I was pumping in him, Sammy managed to put on five pounds of muscle that week. Every two hours, I meted out creatine and fat burners and liquid protein. For breakfast, he got a spoon of oatmeal; for dinner, a sliver of baked fish. At night, I gave him wooden clothes hangers to chew on. "Shit, son, we're mostly powder anyway," I'd tell him whenever he started to cramp. *"South Ohio!"* I screamed every time he puked.

But then, the next Saturday, Sammy didn't show up for the eight o'clock workout. I'd spent the afternoon purging in the bathroom, and somehow he'd slipped away. I walked back to the fridge to get a bottle of Nitro, and discovered the Deca bottle was almost empty—six weeks' worth! The little faggot was going for the easier, softer way, just like his mother always did. I went ahead and did my back and shoulders, then took a shower and got dressed. I had a good idea where he'd run off to, and I wanted to catch the little bastard in the act. My plan was to kick his ass all over Main Street, embarrass the fuck out of him. Nobody disobeyed Luther Colburn. I had twenty-one-inch arms and a fifty-four-inch chest.

By the time I made it down to the main drag, traffic was at a standstill; shit, cars were even backed up onto Route 23. The cold weather had definitely set in, and the sign on the bank read eighteen degrees. I cut back and forth through the alleys until I finally found a spot to park behind Miller's Auto Parts. As soon as I walked around the corner, I spotted him, my stupid son. He was standing across the street under the Mickey D's sign in his posing trunks, a pair of women's panties hanging on his head.

The town was in an uproar, even worse than the week they put on the Farmers' Festival. Bobby Lowe would hit a pose, then Sammy would copy him. Everyone was honking their horns and passing bottles and screaming stupid shit, as if they'd just discovered Elvis beating his meat in their shower stall. Then I saw it. It stretched across his face, gleaming like a toothpaste ad. I'd never realized Sammy could smile like that. It was like seeing his mother all over again. But then, just as I started across the street, dodging the cars and cursing the fucking drivers, he swung around to do a full frontal and dropped to the sidewalk.

I remember kicking him, ordering him to get up, and then some bastard hitting me in the head with something from behind. They were sliding Sammy and me into the ambulance when I came to. He was code blue. As we flew up the highway with the siren wailing and the lights flashing, I watched the paramedic work on him. Sammy was still smiling when the man gave up. "You're shitting me," I said as a chunk of bloody glass fell out of my head and landed on the rubber floor mat. "Do something, goddamn it!"

The paramedic zapped Sammy with the paddles again. Little white sparks flew off his frozen chest. Nothing.

"Jesus Christ, that boy's the next South Ohio," I said, grabbing the man by the throat. "He's got a smile that can beat the world. He can't be dead!" I shut off his air, watched as the veins in his eyes started to burst, and then I suddenly turned him loose. "I'm sorry," I told him, "but that's my boy."

"Really, mister, I did everything I could."

"He's only eighteen years old," I said, kneeling down beside the gurney and running my hand over my son's dead body.

In the ER, some doctor came in the curtained-off room where they were stitching up the back of my head. He laid his hand on my shoulder. "Mr. Colburn, your son suffered a heart attack. He had hypothermia, and his cholesterol was . . ." He glanced down at his clipboard. "Six hundred to be exact. Was he on medication?"

I shook my head. "No, he was healthy as a horse. Shit, you saw him."

"Well, maybe on the outside," the doctor said, staring at me. "Okay, let me ask you this, was he on some type of steroids? We'll get a toxicology report back tomorrow, but do you know anything about it?"

"That's stupid," I said. "Why do you think he was on the juice?"

"Well, besides the needle marks on his legs, he—"

"Fuck off," I said, grabbing my coat. Then I called a taxi and went back to the gym and did stiff-legged dead lifts until I passed out. When I woke up the next morning, I was curled up on the platform with shit in my pants.

After that night, nobody came to the gym anymore, not even Little Ralph, but half the town came to Sammy's funeral. I buried my boy and went back to my routine, wiping down the equipment every day, sweeping the floor, plodding through my workouts. But I kept losing focus; one morning I woke up hanging upside down from the power rack like a bat, all the mirrors covered with old newspapers. A few nights later, I binged on two boxes of candy bars I found stashed under Sammy's cot, then turned around and overdosed on a box of laxatives. The next day I tacked a CLOSED sign to the front door and scattered a box of nails in the parking lot.

A few weeks later, on a Sunday afternoon in early February, the radio started issuing reports about a cold front moving in, warning everyone to stay home. As I listened to predictions about record lows, my head suddenly became as clear as a ziplock baggie. I pulled on some old sweats, ate some aspirin. After sticking a stack of Sammy's Megadeth CDs in the stereo and cranking it up, I just started doing set after set after fucking set. I pumped iron for eight hours straight, a personal best. Then around 2 AM, I took a scorching shower, shaved off all my body hair and greased myself down.

The town was dead when I pulled into the McDonald's parking lot. Beer cans and hamburger wrappers were frozen to the ground. The sign on the bank said two degrees. Little beads of ice were falling out of the sky, and the Christmas lights still hanging in Miller's store popped on and off in the dark windows. I got out of the car and began taking off my clothes. After stripping down to nothing, I stepped over to the spot on the sidewalk where Sammy had fallen.

I started off with some basics, going through them slowly, trying to warm up. Then I went into some secret stuff that I'd been working on for years, shit I was going to show Sammy when he was good enough. The wind cut across my naked body like a meat slicer. Staring across at the bank sign, I kept sucking the icy air and praying for the discipline to hold each pose perfectly. The temperature finally bottomed out at minus thirty-six degrees. My muscles ground against each other like ice floes in the cold silence.

As morning approached, I lifted my frozen arms for one more shot and a loud crack shook the entire valley. A white light exploded in my head and my body shattered into a thousand tiny pieces. Then I blew like flakes of dirty snow down the gray, empty street.

ASSAILANTS

STANDING IN HIS UNDERWEAR IN FRONT OF THE FADED pink duplex that he and Geraldine rented, Del came out of a blackout while taking a leak in the dead August grass. That was the bad thing about coming to: one minute he was like some brainless carp happily munching shit on the bottom of Paint Creek, then *pop*, a flash of light and he was floundering around on dry land again, caught in the middle of another embarrassing fuckup. Lately it seemed to happen every time he got loaded. "Jesus," he said to himself. "Well, at least it ain't the goddamn broom closet." The last time, he'd cut loose in the spoon drawer in the middle of the night after passing out at Geraldine's birthday party. They had been eating with plastic forks ever since.

Del didn't realize that it was still daylight outside until he looked up into the shocked eyes of the two old ladies standing on the sidewalk staring at him. They were close enough to spit on. One of them, tall and thin with a silver beehive hairdo, began gasping for air, her mouth popping open like the trunk of a car, her false teeth ready to leap out and clatter down the street like in some old-time cartoon. The other woman, round and squat, wore a shiny red jogging suit that made her look like a fat tomato. Her pancake makeup was beginning to melt in the heat, and he watched in hungover awe as part of her greasy face suddenly broke loose and slid down her neck just as she started pounding on the back of her wheezing friend. Turning away from them, he lurched toward the porch, warm piss dribbling on his bare feet. And just like that, Del was home.

Geraldine was hiding behind the front door with Veena, their baby, propped on her hip, peering out at her husband through the thin, smoke-stained curtain. She stood there all the time, sucking on menthol cigarettes and watching the street for possible assailants. Six months ago, her old doctor at the Henry J. Hamilton Rehabilitation Center had put her back on all her medications after somebody disguised in a paper bag tried to strangle her in front of the Tobacco Friendly. Though she described the sack perfectly, even drew a picture of it down at the station, the cops never found a single suspect. Nowadays, she wouldn't even stick her hand out the door to check the mailbox.

"I shoulda stayed at the Henry J!" Geraldine cried to Del on the way home from the police station right after the attack. She was in the backseat, frantically trying to burrow into the floorboards with her hands.

"Hey, Geri, you're the one that was beggin' to get out of that damn nuthouse," Del yelled back at her. "You're the one wanted to get married," he pointed out for the hundredth time. He'd first met Geraldine when she was living in the group home over on Fourth Street. Back then she did sex in public places, carried cold fish sticks in her purse the way other people pack chewing gum, handing them out to strangers like precious gifts. Then Del had gotten her pregnant, and in one brave, ecstatic moment, Geraldine flushed all her pills. The next day, she filled out a job application for Del at the plastics factory, conjured up an old wedding ring out of thin air. Now he was stuck.

Del shoved the door open, and Geraldine listed to one side to let him pass. She'd never lost the weight from the baby. "What the hell?" she said. "The whole friggin' neighborhood's watching us, for Christ's sakes." Sickly dark circles surrounded her cloudy eyes like little moats. Sometimes Del envied her; he couldn't get a doctor within fifty miles of Meade, Ohio, to put him on anything.

"I musta been sleepwalkin'," Del mumbled. Then he staggered on and flopped down on the itchy plaid couch. Guns N' Roses was blasting away in the apartment upstairs. The speed-freak nurses from the VA hospital were starting early today. First, they'd get cranked up at home, then go out trolling for men in the bars uptown. Every time they got lucky, Del stared at the ceiling and listened to the squeaking beds above him, half expecting the entire orgy to crash down on his head any second. On those nights, he held his dick in his hand like a holy cross, praying for their hearts to burst into pieces so that he could get some sleep.

He was standing in a green pasture pitching a perfect ringer when Geraldine shook him awake. "Get your ass up," she ordered. "It's your turn to babysit."

Geraldine was still pissed because Del had slipped out that morning while she was in the shower. It was his day off, and they were supposed to attempt a trip to the Columbus Zoo, but at the last minute he decided to flee. He couldn't stand the thought of dealing with Geraldine's panic attacks all the way up Route 23. Her doctor had suggested the trip weeks ago, but she'd kept putting it off, hoping the medication would eventually make the outside world a friendlier place to visit.

Instead Del had driven out to Knockemstiff that morning in the beat-up Cavalier, then spent the better part of the day pitching horseshoes with some of his worthless cousins. "It's cleaner than the last batch," Porter assured him, handing him a joint laced with angel dust. Del hated PCP; it seemed like the gods fucked with him every time he smoked the shit. And sure enough, by the time he headed back to town, some bearded bastard with bad teeth wrapped in a piece of outdoor carpet was popping on and off in the rearview mirror like a beer sign, talking crazy shit about Del's old high school.

"WHAT?" DEL SAID, REARING UP FROM THE COUCH, BLOWing some pillow fuzz out of his mouth. "Where you going?" he asked Geraldine. She'd smeared some lipstick across her face, put some limp curls in her oily hair.

"None of your goddamn business," she spat. "Maybe I'll go to the Topper. How would you like that, you prick?" The Topper sat right across the street from the plastics factory. All the patrons had raw, red faces from the heat of the ovens, splatter burns up and down their arms. No one who drank there was ever completely healed.

"What about Veena?" Del said, looking around on the floor for his pants. He knew his wife wasn't going anywhere; Geraldine hadn't been out of the house in six months.

"She's all yours tonight, daddy," Geraldine said hatefully. "And by the way, where in the fuck did you go this morning?"

"I think I got hold of a green beer."

She stared at him for a few seconds, then said, "You're pathetic, Del, you know that?" She lit a cigarette and stood over him with an ugly sneer on her face. Her crotch was just inches from his nose. "I'll tell you what, buddy boy, you better start paying attention."

"I know, Geri, I know," Del said. Then he added, looking up at her, "I'll do better, I promise." Lately, though, he'd begun wishing for the old days, when he'd only known her as the Fish Stick Girl, and they were bumming spare change at traffic lights. Groaning, he pulled on his jeans and trudged across the hall to Veena's room. He picked her up out of the crib. "She's wet," he yelled.

"Then change her," Geraldine said as she started toward the front door. She was jangling the car keys in her hand, twisting her ass as if she were taking off on some runway in a fashion show. She had on her good jeans, had her big feet crammed into a pair of cheap spiky shoes.

Del laid Veena down gently on the couch and pulled the last diaper out of a Pampers box. There, in the bottom of the carton, lay a small cache of fish sticks wrapped in a greasy paper towel. He stared at the brown, crumbly wafers in disbelief. Geraldine hadn't touched a fish stick since he'd become her legal guardian; it was part of the agreement. He wiped Veena off, sprinkled some baby powder on the raw red rash that covered the insides of her pudgy thighs. Looking at his daughter, Del suddenly felt a great sorrow well up inside him. Falling to his knees, he was just beginning to ask the baby for her forgiveness when he heard his wife tromp back down the hall and slam the bedroom door shut. Both daughter and father jumped at the sound, one still flush with innocence, the other guilty of a thousand trespasses.

After he fed Veena and put her to bed, Del sat in front of the window fan eating slices of white bread and watching the TV with the volume turned low, listening to the nurses party upstairs. He waited impatiently until he figured Geraldine was asleep, then stole the few dollars she had managed to stick in Veena's college-fund jar. Next he filched a couple of her Xanax from the medicine cabinet and swallowed them dry. Slipping out of the house, he jumped in the Cavalier and drove straight over to the Quikstop for a twelve-pack. A shiny new Cadillac was parked right up next to the glass entrance door. A fat man was leaning against the counter checking out the little clerk, his big belly smashing the candy bars on the shelf underneath. The girl was bent over tearing open a carton of cigarettes, nervously chewing on a strand of her long brown hair. Dressed in a pair of white slacks and a silky purple shirt, the man was decorated in gold jewelry, matching chains and bracelets, big rings that twinkled like stars under the fluorescent lights.

As Del approached the counter with his beer, the fat man turned and scowled at him, then stomped out the door. The minty smell of cologne hung in the air where he'd stood. Del watched as he lowered himself daintily into the Caddy. He thought the man looked vaguely familiar, but then all rich people looked the same to him.

"Thanks," the clerk said when Del set the beer down on the counter.

"Huh?"

"See that guy?" she said, nodding toward the window. They both watched as the expensive car slowly pulled out onto the street. "He's in here every night almost," she explained. "Just stands around staring at my butt, offers me money to go out with him. It's creepy."

"I figured him for a queer," Del said. "All that disco shit he's wearing."

"I think he could go either way," she said with a shrug.

"You should hear some of the stuff he talks about." Del looked at the girl. Her name tag said AMY in raised white letters. She had big eyes like funhouse mirrors; a gray metal stud stuck through her tongue like a nail. All the while she was talking, she kept chewing on her hair, rearranging the cigarettes in the case above her head. When he first walked in, Del had figured her for just another speed freak; crank had spread like a virus all over southern Ohio that summer. But suddenly he understood that the fat man was the real reason the girl was so twitchy.

"Call the cops," Del advised.

"Shoot," she snorted, "they're in here every night for the free coffee, but they won't do nothing. They're afraid if they say something, he won't hire their kids for summer help. Heck, I don't even get free coffee."

"What do you mean, hire their kids?" Del asked. "Who is that guy?"

"He's some big shot over at the plastics plant," the girl said. "He's like a millionaire."

Suddenly Del recalled the first time he'd seen the man. Three months ago, a meeting was set up for all the workers to meet the new manager. When they got to the conference room, a TV with a VCR was wheeled in on a little stand. Then the foreman turned on the set and everyone watched the fat man give a speech about productivity. He told them if things didn't pick up, they were all out of a job. He mentioned China, Vietnam, Alabama. The speech lasted fifteen minutes, then the foreman shut off the set and spat on the screen. "Imagine that fat bastard running a press," he said as he rewound the tape. "His candy ass wouldn't last one day." Then he turned and faced the workers. Half of them were already asleep.

"Boys," he said, "you heard what the sonofabitch said. Let's get back to work."

"Well," Del said to the clerk, "he's gone now."

"Oh, he'll be back," she said. "He's like some kind of crazy stalker or something."

"Aw, maybe he just wants to be your boyfriend," Del joked, slipping his wedding ring off and sliding it into his pocket. "Who could blame him for that?"

"That's the other thing," she said excitedly, suddenly pulling her hair out of her mouth. "Guys like to come in here and flirt, you know? But he gets pissed about it. He even ran this one boy off the other night. I couldn't believe it."

"You're kiddin' me," Del said.

"No, I'm serious," she said. "And when I told him to leave, he just laughed at me."

"Jesus, maybe you better be careful," Del said. "Hell, he could be some kind of goddamn sex fiend."

"Don't say that," she said with a shudder. "It's already bad enough being in here at night by myself."

"Hey, I'm serious," Del said. "What about the woman who got attacked down there by the cigarette store? They never did catch that guy."

The clerk gave a little laugh. "Yeah, but that woman was some kind of nutcase, homeless person or something," she said, handing Del his change and sticking the beer in a bag. "She used to come in here with all this rotten food in her purse, trying to give it away. Believe me, she was like totally gross."

His face turning red, Del jammed the pennies and dimes into the pocket of his jeans, then grabbed the beer. He started out the door, but suddenly stopped, his hand frozen on the

metal handle. "That's bullshit, what you just said," he said angrily, his back to the clerk. "That woman? She's married to
some guy I know." He stared out into the illuminated parking
lot, empty except for his old beater. He pushed the door open.
"They even got a little baby," Del added, his voice on the verge
of cracking.

He walked quickly across the lot and got into the Cavalier.
He sat there trembling, thinking about what the girl had said
about Geraldine. "You think you're scared of that fat man, you
just wait," he said out loud. Then, pulling the beer out of the
bag, he tore two ragged eyeholes in the brown paper. He could
see the clerk inside, now sitting on a high stool, her hand
crammed into a bag of Doritos. Taking a deep breath, he
slipped the sack over his head, then jumped out of the car and
raced up to the window. "Hey!" he screamed, slamming his
fists against the plate glass. The startled girl tumbled backward off the stool, banging her head against the sharp corner
of the deli case. Del stood there for a moment in the humid
night, his sour breath trapped in the bag, looking down at the
still figure lying on the tile floor. Then he slipped his wedding
ring back on, walked quickly to his car, and drove home.

RAINY SUNDAY

IT WAS ONE O'CLOCK IN THE MORNING ON A RAINY SUNDAY, and Sharon was sitting at the kitchen table debating whether or not to stuff another slice of American cheese into her mouth when Aunt Joan called, begging her niece to ride into town. "Would you mind we try one more time?" she said. Her voice sounded thick and fuzzy on the phone, and Sharon figured she had been taking somebody else's pills again. Ever since her father died, Aunt Joan had been working in a nursing home in Meade, changing diapers and spooning soft food into the mouths of old people who'd worn out their welcome in this world. She considered their medication one of the perks of the job.

Sharon pulled back the curtain and looked out the window. In the glow from the security light, she could see water standing several inches deep on the road in front of the house. "Lord, woman," she told her aunt, "it's still pouring down out there." She didn't want to go outside again. Earlier that day, she had gotten soaked chasing Dean, her damaged husband, around the yard. Now her throat hurt and she could feel a cold coming on. Sharon dreaded wet weather more than anything.

"Please, honey, I'm so lonely tonight," Aunt Joan said. "I cross my heart, I won't ask you again."

Sharon sighed. She had told her aunt the last time that she wasn't doing it anymore. Not only was it dangerous, it made her feel dirty. Besides, if Dean ever found out, she would never cash another one of his social security checks again. But tonight she couldn't think straight. Dean had the TV turned up full blast in the living room, listening to some big-mouth preacher with frizzy blond hair stuck up around his head like a halo, and no matter where Sharon went in the cramped house, she couldn't escape the sounds of televised religion. Everything was either pearly gates or boiling pits. So with Dean flapping his arms like an angel trying to fly through the ceiling and the preacher pleading for more money and Aunt Joan promising it was just the one more time, she caved in. "Look, this is the last time," Sharon said. "Are you sure you can drive?"

"I'll be there in ten minutes," Aunt Joan said, her voice already perking up. "And, honey, don't wear that stupid ball cap. I need you looking nice."

Sharon hung up the phone and peeled the plastic wrap off one more slice of the waxy cheese. She yelled again at Dean to turn the TV down. Then she went into the bathroom and started putting on her face. In the last year, she had picked up five men for her aunt, but according to the older woman, not one of them had even stuck around for a sausage-and-gravy breakfast the next morning. When Sharon pressed her for details, she clammed up, refused to talk. It was hopeless. Though only in her forties, Aunt Joan wore old-lady dresses that hung like tired sheets on her fat body, and rubber galoshes over her black orthopedic shoes, even in dry weather. Her gray hair was piled on top of her head in a knot the size of a softball, and she had never tasted lipstick in her life. Sharon was heavy, too, but over the years she had learned the secrets of makeup application and how to camouflage her thick body with brightly colored sweats. It wasn't that hard to keep a man if you took care of yourself.

Just as she was finishing her eyes, Sharon heard Dean yell something about a giant turtle and run out the back door. She was too tired and discouraged to go after him, even though she hated for anyone to see him when he was having one of his episodes, especially her aunt. By the time Aunt Joan pulled in the driveway, he was hacking away with a chop ax at the tall TV antenna propped against the side of the house. "My God," Aunt Joan said as Sharon got in the car. "What in the world's he doing now?"

"Who knows?" Sharon said. She crammed some empty pop cans and fast-food containers under the seat to make room for her feet. "This rain's got him all screwed up."

As they started to town, she waited for her aunt to begin her usual speech about marrying a man with a steel plate in his head, but instead, Aunt Joan began telling stories about her sister, Bessie, Sharon's mother. "All the kids in Knockemstiff used to call me and your mom the Cave Women when we were growing up." Sharon had heard most of Aunt Joan's stories a hundred times, and she hated them all, especially this one. The image of some hairy, stooped, apelike creatures always came to mind. "Your mama, though," Aunt Joan said, staring through the cracked windshield of the New Yorker at the dark, wet road, "she didn't deserve all that name-calling, being compared with me. She was pretty, just like you."

"Yeah," Sharon said, "but look how she ended up." Sharon

bummed a Kool off her aunt, thinking the menthol might soothe her throat. "Maybe you were better off in the long run."

"What? Being the ugly one? Slaving away for Daddy all those years?" Aunt Joan said. She rubbed her nose, wiped something on her coat. "No, I don't think so. At least your mom, she had some fun." Most everyone in the county had heard of Big Bessie. She had left home as soon as she turned eighteen and tended bar around Meade all her life. Men fell in love with her face and tried to imagine a different, slimmer body when they bedded her. One night she didn't come home from work, but Sharon just assumed she'd gone off with one of her trucker boyfriends. Bessie would do that once in a while, after Sharon was old enough to look after herself, just up and quit a job and take off for Florida or Texas for a couple of weeks. She'd been gone only three days when Sharon got a call from a detective in Milton, West Virginia. Her mother's body had been found in a Dumpster behind a pancake house. Even now, ten years later, Aunt Joan still called the police department down there to see if they'd made an arrest yet.

"I miss her so much," Aunt Joan said.

As they approached the cement bridge in Knockemstiff that ran over the little creek called Shady Glen, Sharon said, "Be careful."

"Oh, you always say that," Aunt Joan said with a laugh, but she tapped the brakes anyway.

"I know, but I can't help it." She didn't trust anyone's driving anymore. Dean had crashed his car into the bridge four years ago, just before he and Sharon were supposed to get married. Some people he'd gone to vocational school with had thrown him a bachelor party, and the highway patrol estimated Dean was going eighty miles an hour when he flew through the windshield. The next morning, after the last of

the emergency people had pulled away, one of the Myers boys
from up in the holler found a pair of black panties and a sliver
of pink brain in the grass. Nobody dreamed he would live, but
eight months later he walked out of the rehab center on
crutches. A thin layer of skin they'd peeled off his ass covered
the steel plate in the back of his head. Sharon still thought
about the panties occasionally, tried to picture the girl who
wore a size five. She hadn't worn underwear that small since
she was in the third grade.

"I THINK YOU WAITED TOO LONG," SHARON SAID AS THEY
drove slowly past the dark Tecumseh Lounge. It was the
last dive her mother had worked in. The owner still had a
photograph of Big Bessie on the wall behind the cash register.
Twice, she and Aunt Joan had gotten lucky there.

"Damn, I was hoping we'd beat last call," Aunt Joan said.
"The drunks, they're the easiest." She pulled the car over at
the edge of the empty parking lot and hunted in her purse for
a fresh pack of cigarettes. The rain, which had practically
stopped on the long drive into town, started up again. Sharon
wondered if Dean had found his way back inside the house.
"Oh, well," Aunt Joan sighed. "What about we go get some
doughnuts? I always got a sweet tooth, don't you?"

Besides the cross-eyed waitress, there was only one other
person in the Crispie Creme, a wasted-looking young man in
a booth near the back who seemed to be talking to himself. As
they stood waiting for their order at the glass counter, Aunt
Joan whispered that he was the same guy who'd been in there
the last time they'd come to town. "Remember?" she said. "He
was with some guy had a split-looking mouth."

"Maybe," Sharon said.

"He looks lonely."

The man glanced up from his cup, then squinted at them in the bright fluorescent lighting. He stuck out his coffee-stained tongue. "You're kidding, right?" Sharon said.

"What do you mean?"

"Christ, Aunt Joan, he looks like a friggin' serial killer."

"He don't look no worse than the other ones, Sharon. Besides, I don't figure we're gonna find any movie stars out this late." She counted out the exact change for the silent waitress. "C'mon, let's sit."

"Goddamn it," Sharon muttered under her breath. She had hoped maybe her aunt would forget about finding one tonight. With their hot chocolates and the box of doughnuts, they sat down in a booth across from the man. He nodded and batted his bloodshot eyes, showed them a mouthful of yellow teeth. Aunt Joan gave him a shy smile, then kicked Sharon's shin until her niece finally asked the man to sit with them.

He told them his name was Jimmy as he eagerly slid into the booth next to Sharon. His greasy hair hung down in his eyes and a patchy beard covered his skinny neck. Faded blue letters decorated the knuckles of each hand. Aunt Joan did most of the talking, asking him bullshit questions about his family origins, bitching about the rainy weather. Sharon knew she was sizing him up, trying to decide if he might be a man she wouldn't mind waking up next to in the morning. For his part, Jimmy just kept repeating the same phrases over and over; "Cool" and "Party time" seemed to be the only words he knew. It was obvious to Sharon that he didn't have a brain in his head. Her aunt would think he was perfect.

Aunt Joan finally nodded at Sharon and excused herself. They watched her walk back to the restroom, and Sharon hoped to God that she'd never waddle like that. Jimmy scooted up against her and suggested that they dump the old cow, but Sharon ignored him. By the time Aunt Joan returned, he had his arm wrapped around her niece, his tongue stuck in her ear. Five minutes later, they were all getting into the car. "You two go ahead and sit in the back," Aunt Joan said. "I'll handle the driving."

As soon as they backed out of the parking lot, Jimmy pulled a plastic bag and a spray can from his coat pocket. "Party time," he said again, nudging Sharon with his elbow. She watched him fill the bag with spray, then stick his face in it and inhale deeply several times. Whatever it was smelled like ether and she rolled her window down despite the rain. He finally let the can drop to the floor and leaned back in the seat. A glob of spit dripped off his dirty beard. His eyes became as vacant as a dead TV. Sharon looked up and saw her aunt smiling at her in the rearview mirror.

Whatever he sniffed didn't last long, and as soon as Jimmy came out of his fog, Aunt Joan leaned across the seat and opened the glove box. She took out a pint of whiskey, made a big deal out of twisting the cap off and pretending to take a hit. At the last red light in Meade, she handed the bottle back to him. He took a drink and offered it to Sharon. She shook her head, told him she'd already drank too much hot chocolate. He and Aunt Joan passed the bottle back and forth several times, and every time Jimmy took another drink, he pushed his hand farther down inside Sharon's sweatpants. Finally Aunt Joan said, "Sharon, I'll bet your boyfriend can't kill the rest of that bottle."

Jimmy held the pint up and looked at it. "Lady, you don't know ol' Jimmy very well, do you?" he said. As he raised the bottle to his mouth, Sharon saw her aunt reach over and turn the heater on high. Warm air filled the car. When he finished chugging, Jimmy smacked his lips and said, "I could do that all night long." Then he slipped his tongue in Sharon's ear again. Just as she began to tingle a little bit, his hand quit moving inside her pants. She jerked it out and he fell back against the door, mumbling something about fat girls being tight.

"Okay," Sharon said as she wiped spit out of her ear. "Stop the car."

"What's wrong?" Aunt Joan flipped on her turn signal, and began slowing down.

"Ain't nothing wrong," Sharon said. "But I'm not sitting back here all the way home. He smells like a medicine cabinet."

Easing the car over to the side of the highway, Aunt Joan asked, "What was that stuff anyway?"

Sharon felt around on the floorboards until she found the can. She held it up to the light from a passing car. "Bactine," she said. "Yeah, Aunt Joan, you sure know how to pick 'em."

"Throw it out. They say that stuff will rot your brain sniffing it like that."

"It's already too late for this one," Sharon said as she got in the front seat and slammed the door shut. "Mr. Party Time. Ha. He's a pig."

Aunt Joan laughed. "Oh, don't talk about my new man like that. He might end up being a keeper." A semi blew past them just before Aunt Joan pulled the big car back onto the highway.

"It ain't funny," Sharon shouted. "He had his hand clear up inside me."

"Eat one of those doughnuts."

"I don't want no doughnut. I just want to go home."

"Honey, this is the last time, I promise," Aunt Joan said.

Sharon lit a cigarette just as the car engine started making a hammering sound. The New Yorker had been practically new when Aunt Joan's daddy gave it to her three years ago, but she never took care of anything. John Grubb had traded his pickup in on the car the same day the doctors told him that his diabetes had scored another victory. Your legs this time, they had told him. He'd already lost most of his toes. On the way out of town with the new car, he stopped at Jack's Hardware and bought a ten-gallon cowboy hat and a .45 pistol that came with a fancy shoulder holster. Then he drove back to the farmhouse he shared with his youngest daughter and wired a cow's skull to the front grille of the car. For the next two months, he drove around the county drinking whiskey and eating bags of hardtack candy and listening to Jerry Lee Lewis cassettes. Sharon knew the story by heart; her aunt told it every time the car broke down.

They were halfway home when Aunt Joan tapped Sharon on the leg and said, "Honey, check on that boy, will you?"

Sharon groaned and twisted around in her seat. Though it was dark in the car, she thought she could see one of Jimmy's eyes open, like a shiny coin, staring up at her. Getting up on her knees, she leaned over the front seat and lit her cigarette lighter. Both of his eyes flickered. She'd never seen that before. "What was in that bottle?" she said.

"Same as last time," Aunt Joan said. "Those Percocets I been getting off old Mrs. Marsh."

"Well, his friggin' eyes are open," Sharon said.

"Is he doing anything else? Is he moving?"

"No, but his goddamn eyes are awake."

Aunt Joan was silent for a moment. "Burn him with your Zippo a little."

"Are you nuts?"

"Oh, don't set him on fire. Just see if he flinches is all."

Sharon looked closely at Jimmy one more time, then

dropped back down in her seat and said, "Aunt Joan, I ain't doing that." The clattering sound under the hood finally eased up, and Sharon tried to relax. She leaned her head back and watched the wipers flop loosely back and forth across the windshield. Her grandfather had finally returned home when his eyes gave out from the sugar and he couldn't see to drive anymore. Hobbling into the house on his rotten legs, he gave his daughter a peck on the cheek and handed her both sets of keys. "Joanie, that's a good car," he told her. "Take care of it." John Grubb had always kept his youngest daughter close, so close that people around the holler had spread rumors, and it had only gotten worse after Edna was killed. But while she was peeling potatoes for his dinner, he slipped out on the back porch and blew a hole behind his ear with the .45. She was forty-three years old and had never been on a date.

They turned off the highway onto Black Run, the secondary road that would take them back to the holler. "Do I have to help you carry him in?" Sharon asked.

Aunt Joan rubbed her chin, turned down the heater. "No, I don't reckon," she said. "You've done enough."

Ten minutes later, she stopped the car in front of Sharon's house. They could both see Dean pacing back and forth in the front room, jabbing his hands into the air. All the lights were on. It looked like a hundred people lived there. Pieces of the TV antenna were scattered in the muddy driveway. "Where's your curtains?" Aunt Joan asked.

"I have no friggin' idea," Sharon said numbly. It was four o'clock in the morning, and Dean had been at it since yesterday afternoon when the rain started. He'd been to doctors all over Ohio, but nobody could explain why the rain made him so crazy.

"You're going to have to do something about that boy one of these days," Aunt Joan said. "He's going to have one of those fits and hurt somebody."

Sharon rolled her eyes. At least she had a regular man. "That last doctor he saw told us to try moving to the desert," she said, watching her husband through the naked windows.

"The desert?" Aunt Joan said. "You mean with camels and sheikhs and stuff?"

"No, like Arizona."

"Oh." Aunt Joan got a serious look on her face. Reaching over, she took hold of her niece's hand and squeezed it. "Sharon," she said, staring into her eyes, "Dean ain't worth moving away for, you hear me?" She turned and looked back at the house. "He gets to where you can't handle him, we can take care of that."

Aunt Joan was always suggesting that Sharon do something about Dean, either divorce him or stick him in a group home. Putting up with her advice had been more of an aggravation than anything else. Tonight though, as she listened to Jimmy's soggy wheeze in the backseat, Sharon thought about the other men they had brought back to the holler, wondered again why Aunt Joan refused to talk about them.

Aunt Joan shrugged. "I'm just saying I wouldn't want to live in no desert."

Sharon started to get out of the car. "Don't worry, that's just what the head doctor said."

"Here, you take these," Aunt Joan said, handing Sharon the box of doughnuts.

"I thought you had a sweet tooth."

"I do," the older woman chuckled. She turned and glanced back at Jimmy. "But not for no doughnuts."

Walking in the house, Sharon saw that Dean had not only torn all the curtains down, but he'd smashed every pretty thing she had hanging on the walls. "You're gonna clean this up, mister," she told him. A confused look clouded his face, and he curled up on the couch and started scratching the back of his head. He dug harder and harder into his scalp until she had to run over and grab his arms. The thin piece of skin over the steel plate was raw and bleeding. He calmed down for a few moments, then jumped up and started singing "Row, Row, Row Your Boat" at the top of his froggy voice.

Sharon gave up and went around shutting off all the lights. A photograph of her and Dean lay on the floor in the kitchen, the frame broken, and she kicked it under the table. Then she walked down the hallway and unlocked her bedroom door with a key she kept on a chain around her neck. Pulling off her sweats, she crawled into bed with the box of doughnuts and pulled the blankets up over her. Yes, she thought, she was definitely catching a cold. She turned on the little radio that sat on the nightstand and twisted the dial until she found some easy-listening music.

Taking a doughnut from the box, Sharon bit into it, a chocolate cream filled. Raindrops splattered against the window. She ate the doughnut and wondered what it would be like to live in the desert. Everything there would be new. She could go on a diet and Dean could get his head dried out. They could do whatever people do who live in the sand.

Biting into a glazed, she started to think about Jimmy. He'd stuck his tongue in her ear, the first time anyone had ever done that. His breath was bad, but so was Dean's. She wished now that she'd asked him, when they were in the backseat together, if he'd ever been to Arizona. She wondered if he had a girlfriend, maybe even a wife. She hadn't noticed a wedding ring, but that didn't mean anything these days. Then she remembered Aunt Joan and decided that she better not think about Jimmy anymore. Besides, she was done with all that business now.

Sharon licked the sugary coating off her fingers and picked up a blueberry, one of her favorites. Through the door, she heard Dean moving around again. Then the DJ came on and said something about more precipitation. She reached over and turned the radio up a little. The rain had settled, the man said in his late-night voice, over the Ohio valley. It was going to stick around a while.

HOLLER

I WOKE UP THINKING I'D PISSED THE BED AGAIN, BUT IT WAS just a sticky spot from where Sandy and me fucked the night before. Those kinds of things happen when you drink like I do—you shit your pants in the Wal-Mart, you end up living off some crackhead and her poor parents. I raised the blankets just a tad, traced my finger over the blue KNOCKEM-STIFF, OHIO tattoo that Sandy had etched in her skinny ass like a road sign. Why some people need ink to remember where they come from will always be a mystery to me.

Wrapping my arms around her, I pulled Sandy up against me, blew my bad breath on the back of her neck. I was just getting ready to nail her again when Sandy's dad started up down the hall in his sickroom, crying soft and sad like he'd been doing ever since his stroke. That pretty much drained the sap out of me. Sandy groaned and rolled away to the other side of the bed, covered her blond head with a lumpy pillow that was crusty with dried sex and slobber.

I stared at the ceiling and listened as Mary, Sandy's mom,

trudged past the door on her way to check on Albert. The cold floorboards cracked and creaked like ice under her fat legs. Everything in the house seemed old and used up, and that included Sandy. It was just like what my old man always claimed about my mother after she took off—"If she had all of 'em stickin' out of her that's been stuck in her, she'd look like a fuckin' porcupine." That was Sandy all right; damn near every boy in Twin Township had tapped her one time or another.

Through the thin walls, I heard Mary tell her bedridden husband, "No, he ain't up yet." Ever since Sandy brought me home with her one night last fall, I'd been helping take care of Albert. Each morning, before Mary would crack his first fifth of wine, I'd go in and shave the old man, scrub him off, change his diaper. It all came down to a matter of timing. If Albert didn't get his breakfast by ten o'clock, he'd start seeing dead soldiers hanging from parachutes in the apple tree outside his window. This meant getting up early, but I kept thinking that if I did right by the old man, maybe somebody would return the favor someday. I rose up and looked at the clock on the dresser.

Pulling on my jeans, I glanced down at some of Sandy's pencil drawings scattered on the floor. She was always working on a picture of the Ideal Boyfriend. Sometimes she'd fire up some ice and lock herself in the room, stay revved up for two or three nights practicing different body parts. Reams of her fantasy were slid under the bed. Not a damn one of those pictures looked like me, and I suppose I should have been grateful for that. Every one of them had the same tiny head, the same cannonball shoulders. Eventually, she'd crawl out of the room with blisters on her fingers from squeezing the pencil, scabs around her mouth from smoking the shit.

Albert started smacking his flaky white lips as soon as I entered the room. Except for a constant tremor in his left hand, he was dead as Jesus from the chest down. Mary had already retreated to the living room, but she'd put out a dishpan of warm water and a thin towel on the stand next to the hospital bed. A can of Gillette and a straight razor sat on top of the dresser. I lathered him up and lit a cigarette to steady my nerves. I studied the map of veins on his purple nose while he grinned at me through the foam.

Just as I began scraping his neck, Mary rushed through the door with a fifth of Wild Irish Rose. Albert's head started trembling as soon as his yellow eyes zoomed in on the wine. "It's nearly ten, Tom," Mary panted. "You about done?"

"Almost," I answered, flicking some ashes on the floor. "Maybe you oughta go ahead and give him a hit. He gets to bouncin' around, I might cut him."

Mary shook her head. "Not 'til ten o'clock," she said adamantly. "We start that, it'll just get earlier and earlier. He runs me ragged as it is."

"I still gotta change him, though," I said, pressing my palm against his sweaty forehead to keep him still. "What about his medication? Maybe you ought to try it sometime."

"This *is* his medication," Mary said, waving the bottle around. "Lord, he wouldn't last a day without it." There was a drawer full of pills in the nightstand, but in all the months I'd been staying there, I was the only one who took anything his doctor had prescribed.

I finished the shave job, then wiped Albert's face with a damp washcloth, ran a comb through his brittle gray hair. Pulling down the scratchy blankets, I said, "You ready, pardner?" His face twisted as he tried to spit out a few garbled words, and then he gave up and nodded his head. The old man hated me changing him, but it was better than lying in his squirts all day. I unfastened the paper diaper and took a deep breath, then raised his bony legs up with one hand and pulled it out from under him. It was soaked with brown goo. I dropped it in the wastebasket, wiped his ass with the washcloth. Then I taped a new diaper on him from the box of Adult Pampers lying on the floor. By the time I had him fixed up, he was bawling again.

As soon as I tucked the blankets back up around him, Mary broke the seal on the bottle and handed it to me. I jabbed one end of a straw down the neck of the jug, slipped the other end in Albert's mouth. The clock on the wall said 9:56. Four more minutes and he would have been back in Korea. I held the fifth and smoked another cigarette while the old man sucked down his morning oats. Sandy's high, whiny voice traveled down the hallway into the sickroom. She was singing her song about a blue bird that wanted to be a red bird. "Where'd you two go last night?" Mary asked.

"Hap's," I said, dabbing at a trickle of wine running off Albert's chin.

"I should have figured," she said, and left the room. Other than Hap's Bar, the only other business that was still hanging on in Knockemstiff was Maude Speakman's store. Even the church had fallen on tough times. Nobody had loyalty anymore. Everyone wanted to work in town and make the big money at the paper mill or the plastics factory. They preferred doing their shopping and praying in Meade because the prices were lower and the churches were bigger. I figured it was only a matter of time before Hap Collins sold his liquor license to the highest bidder and closed up the only good thing still left in the holler.

After Albert nodded off, I killed the inch of dregs he'd left in the bottle, then went out to the kitchen and poured a cup of coffee. From the back window, I could see all the way across Knockemstiff. It had snowed a bit during the night, and smoke rose from the chimneys of the shotgun houses and rust-streaked trailers scattered along the gravel road below. A chain saw started up somewhere over Slate Hill. I ate a piece of cold toast while watching Porter Watson fill his truck with gas at Maude's, then stumble across the parking lot in all his camouflage padding and go inside the store.

Looking across to the other end of the holler, I could just make out the frosted nose of the Owl's car sticking out of the hillside across from Hap's Bar. It was an abandoned 1966 Chrysler Newport, but people around here called it the Owl's ride, the Owl's castle, the Owl's this and that. Nothing was known about the car's original owner, but Porter Watson made sure nobody in the fucking county ever forgot the screech owl that had roosted in the front seat the summer after the car, plates missing and engine busted, mysteriously appeared parked halfway up the hill. You'd have thought they were cousins the way Porter went on about that stupid bird.

I rinsed my cup and walked into the living room, eased myself down into the saggy couch. Scenic vistas torn from old calendars were pinned to the walls, looking like windows into other worlds. Triple A guidebooks were scattered everywhere. Though Mary had never owned a car, she had a book for every state. She was always pretending a trip somewhere.

"She's nuts," Sandy had told me the first night I went home with her. We'd just knocked one off and were lying in bed drinking our last quart of beer. "She laid a goddamn rock on my bed the other morning, claimed she'd found it at the Grand Canyon. Kept blowing off she wanted to bring me home something special."

"So?" I'd said.

"So? I'd just watched her pick it up out of the driveway. Hell, that old bitch ain't never been out of the state of Ohio, Tom."

I kept my mouth shut, sucked down the suds in the bottom of the bottle. My wife had finally kicked me out, and I was desperate for a place to stay.

"Besides," Sandy said, getting up and heading for the bathroom, "what kind of present is an old dirty rock anyways?"

WE WATCHED THE TUBE ALL THAT WINTER DAY, SMOKING cigarettes and drinking weak coffee and eating cheese crackers from a box. With the house sitting on top of the knob like it did, the TV could pull in four channels, so there was always something to watch. Still, there were times I wished they had cable. During the commercials, Sandy worked on another drawing of the Ideal Boyfriend, and Mary flipped through a book about Florida. Every so often I'd get up and check on Albert, give him another straw of wine to keep the war away.

Then, right after dusk, Mary ran out of smokes. I watched her out of the corner of my eye as she ransacked drawers, looked under cushions. Finally, she straightened up and went down the hall talking to herself. When she came back, she held out a wrinkled twenty and asked us to go buy her a carton. Sandy grabbed the money and jumped up, ran back to her bedroom. "The store will be closin' before long," Mary yelled. "You don't need to fix up just to go to Maude's."

I knew we were in for it as soon as Sandy pranced back out to the living room. She was wearing lipstick and her tightest jeans; she'd combed the rat's nest out of her hair. The bitter scent of the perfume I'd bought her for Christmas cut through the stale air. Mary's eyes clouded over with worry, but she didn't have any choice. She hadn't walked the hill in a coon's age, and she couldn't go without her smokes. I pulled my coat on and followed her daughter out into the winter darkness. It was the first time we'd been outside all day. "This must be how vampires feel," I said, looking up at the stars through the bare branches of the trees.

"Huh?" Sandy said as she started to trot down the hill ahead of me.

"Slow down," I said. The gravel was icy from where all the cars had packed down the snow. "What's your hurry?"

"I'm thirsty," Sandy said.

"Girl, I ain't got no money."

She turned around, pulled the twenty out of her pocket, and waved it in my face. "I do," she said with a laugh.

"Don't you think we oughta get your mom them cigarettes?"

"Don't worry about it," she said. "She smokes too much anyway."

I KNEW ALL ALONG WE'D NEVER LAST, BUT WHEN I CAME OUT of the john at Hap's and found Sandy gone, I still felt a sick feeling in my stomach. We'd been drinking the cheap draft and listening to her favorite Phil Collins for a couple of hours when she ditched me. I went outside and hunted for her in the parking lot, then came back in and sat down at the bar next to Porter Watson. "You see where Sandy went?" I asked Wanda, the barmaid. My voice was trembling, and I lit my last cigarette with shaky hands.

Wanda set another draft in front of me. "As soon as you hit the pisser, she left out the door with that logger that was in here," she said. "Hell, they'd been eyeing each other since you two got here."

"The Ideal Boyfriend," I muttered.

"The idy what?" Porter asked, turning toward me. His bushy beard smelled like stomach acid.

"Nothing," I said, staring down at the mug of beer. I started to pick it up but then pushed it back toward Wanda. "I ain't got no money," I said.

"I already poured it," Wanda said.

"I'll buy," Porter told her, throwing a five on the bar.

And so I sat there until closing time, drinking on Porter and listening to him go on and on about the Owl's car. When you first heard him talking about it, you'd figure he was bat-shit crazy, but really, he was just trying to latch on to something that would fill up his days so he didn't have to think about what a fucking mess he had made of everything. It's the same for most of us; forgetting our lives might be the best we'll ever do.

"I'd still like to know the history of that car," I said, just to show him I was still listening.

"History?" Porter snorted. "Man, that car's like part of the landscape. It's like fuckin' nature."

"No," I said, "I mean, like, how you figure it got there in the first place?"

"It landed there."

"Landed?" I looked over at him. His bloodshot eyes were locked on the wavy mirror behind the bar. "You mean like . . ."

"Hell, yes," he said. "And we're damn lucky it did," he added, a sob starting to erupt from deep inside his throat.

A few minutes later, Wanda yelled, "Last call!" I looked over at the Miller Beer clock above the door. It said 1:00 AM. Then I remembered the old lady's cigarettes. I couldn't go back to the house without some Marlboros. Hell, she probably wouldn't let me in. I waited until Wanda started to flick the lights off and on, then hit Porter up for the money to get a pack, hoping that would pacify Mary until morning.

"Last call!" Wanda yelled again, as I dropped eight quarters in the cigarette machine.

WHEN I FINALLY MADE IT BACK TO SANDY'S HOUSE, THE gray light of the TV still glowed through the sheets of plastic stapled over the windows. I knocked on the door and watched through the glass as Mary struggled out of the recliner and slowly made her way across the room. Her blue fuzzy housecoat fit her round body like a cocoon. Her pockets bulged with wads of used Kleenex. Pulling the door open, she peered past me into the darkness. "Where's Sandy?" she asked.

"I ain't sure," I said, my teeth chattering from the cold. "She took off."

"What about my cigarettes?"

"I brought you a pack," I said, holding them up to the porch light. "Sandy's got the rest of them."

"That girl," she said, unlatching the screen door. "She don't have the sense to pound sand down a rat hole."

I stepped into the cramped living room, shrugged off my coat. *The Love Boat* was playing on the tube. "Jesus," I said, "I ain't seen that show since I don't know when." It had been one of my mom's favorites, though I always felt it was bullshit, the way everyone fell in love and got what they wanted in the happy ending.

We stood in the middle of the living room staring down at the TV. "I'd give anything to take one of them cruises," Mary said, as she peeled open the pack of smokes.

"Where is that?" I asked. It all looked so beautiful on the

screen, the tropical scenery, the sexy bikinis, the sparkling blue water, even the bald captain in the tuxedo.

"Hawaii," Mary answered. "I seen this one a dozen times. See that woman standing by the rail? The poor thing don't know her hubby's on the ship with his new girlfriend." Mary dropped down into her recliner, lit a cigarette. The tip of the Marlboro began to glow like a stoplight in the middle of her wrinkled face.

"Is that them?" I said. Two has-been movie stars were strolling on the deck, their arms wrapped around each other, their smiling faces pointed up at the sun.

"Yep," Mary said. "The shit's gonna hit the fan pretty soon."

AFTER A FEW MINUTES, MARY NODDED OFF IN HER CHAIR. Taking one of the cigarettes from the pack I'd brought her, I went into the kitchen. I stood by the window smoking and wondering if Sandy and her logger were somewhere fucking right at that moment, their two hearts pounding against each other like sledgehammers while mine barely beat at all. Suddenly, I remembered Albert. I pulled a fifth of Rose from the refrigerator and walked down the hall to check on him. Though it was against Mary's rule, I figured he could do with a snort. A nightlight plugged into an outlet above him shone on his face like a pale blue star. Sitting down beside him, I uncapped the bottle. "Hey, old man," I whispered, "let's have a drink."

I stuck the straw down into the bottle before I realized that Albert was dead. It was probably the first time he'd ever turned down a drink in his life. I sat beside him for a while sipping from his jug and thinking about Sandy. Sometime to-morrow she'd roll in, and I made up my mind I didn't want to be around for that. My job was done here anyway. I turned on the lamp and rummaged through the drawer of pills, found the bottle of Demerol. Then I leaned over, and as gently as I could, pushed Albert's dry, pink eyelids down with my thumbs.

Going back out to the living room, I pulled on my coat and slipped the bottle of wine in my pocket. As I headed for the front door, I looked down and saw one of Sandy's drawings lying on the coffee table. She'd printed WANTED in bold letters over the man's shrunken head. I stuck it in my other pocket, then tiptoed over and gently pried the pack of cigarettes from Mary's hand, leaving her three in the ashtray.

I stood outside the old house for a moment, and then started down the road. As the cold air quickly seeped through my coat, I realized I'd never make it out of the holler tonight. All of Knockemstiff was asleep, even the dogs, and I had no place to go. By the time I got to Hap's cinder-block building, I was damn near frozen. I stood shivering in the middle of the road trying to decide what to do, then leaped over the drainage ditch and scrambled up the hillside. The briars and brush ripped my skin and tore my clothes, but I finally made it to the Owl's car.

I pulled open the rusty door and crawled inside the Newport. I flicked my lighter and looked around. Dirty gray feathers lay everywhere; dry, pale droppings caked the faded cloth seat. I heard a scrunching sound like dried twigs under my boots. Holding the Zippo near my feet, I saw the thin white bones of small animals scattered on the floorboards. It occurred to me that these were probably some of the Owl's victims. I rolled the stubborn windows up as far as they would go and hunkered down in the seat, with just my eyes above the cracked dash.

After finishing off Albert's bottle and popping two of his Demerol, I stretched out as best I could across the front seat. I closed my eyes and sank deeper and deeper into that lonely world known only to those who sleep in abandoned vehicles. As a car rattled past on the road below, I recalled the story about Sandy's uncle Wimpy Miller freezing to death in a Dumpster behind the Sack N' Save, his body buried in out-dated lettuce. Then I thought of Hawaii, tried my best to con-jure up the hot sand of a tropical beach, the warm silky nights of paradise.

The wind picked up, rocking the old car back and forth. Flakes of snow blew through the cracks and swirled above me. Reaching down, I picked up the tiny skull of a wretched little bird. I held it in my hand for a long time. It seemed as if every-thing I'd ever done in my life, the good and the bad, rested there. Then I slipped it, as thin and fragile as an egg, into my mouth.

I START OVER

EVERYBODY'S SEEN IT, THE COMMERCIAL WHERE THE OLD man is running along the moonlit beach with the beautiful pink-haired starlet clad in the silver thong; the one that says it's never too late to start over. This guy's bounding along like a fucking gazelle, his feet barely touching the sand, a bulge the size of a sledgehammer knocking around inside his plaid swimsuit; and then this young girl, she can barely keep up he's moving so fast. It's bullshit, another lie they tease you with, hoping you'll fall for the special effects, dial the toll-free number with a credit card clenched between your false teeth. And it's like all those other artsy commercials nowadays, where they don't actually tell you what they're selling. I mean, they might have a little drama going on about an elephant and a sunflower, but then someone figures out it's just an ad for sanitary napkins, that sort of thing.

But still, they suck you in, this new way they tell a story. The bastards prey on your regrets, divine all your little sorrows. Take me for example, Big Bernie Givens. I'm fifty-six years old and sloppy fat and stuck in southern Ohio like the smile on a dead clown's ass. My wife shudders every time I mention the sex act. My grown son eats the dead stuff that collects on windowsills. I must watch that damn commercial twenty times a day. I dream about it at night, about starting over. I wake up with that background music knocking holes in my heart. Like I said, it's bullshit.

"WHAT'S THOSE THINGS WHERE THEY BURN YOUR DEAD body?" I ask my wife. We're inching forward in the drive-through line at Fedder's Dairy Queen, sucking car fumes and listening to Jerry thrash around in the backseat like an ape caught in a net. It's been the worst summer on record, just one massive heatstroke. My new white shirt is already stained the color of pus; my shades are fogged over with greasy vapors. Fumes from the paper-mill stack across town make the whole county smell like a giant fart. The sun is everywhere.

"Crematorium?" she yawns. She rubs her eyes, runs a freckled hand through her thin brown hair, dead as straw now from too many dye jobs.

"No, not that, like over in Asia," I say, wiping the sweat from my forehead. I should have gone ahead and driven the air-conditioned Mercury today, left the Chevy covered up in the garage. Glancing in the rearview mirror, I watch Jerry struggle against the plastic webbing we use to hold him down and keep him from jumping out into traffic. Blue veins thick as fingers bulge in his scarlet neck. The poor bastard never lets up.

"Shit, how should I know?" Jill groans. She begins fanning

herself with a wrinkled map of Ohio she's dug out of the glove box.

"That's it," I say. "That's what it feels like."

LATELY, I'VE BEEN FUCKING UP LEFT AND RIGHT. THE other night on my way home, I even tried to pick up some young girl. She was walking along Third Street and I drove past first, checking her out. I could see that she was junior high, but I whipped around the block anyway, then pulled over to the curb. "Hey, you need a ride?" I asked. As soon as the words spilled out of my mouth, my teeth started chattering, even though the sign on the bank said it was ninety-two degrees.

The girl looked up and down the street, then edged closer to the car. "Where you going?" she asked. Her voice sounded like tinfoil. Pictures of butterflies covered her pink shirt. She had the body of a woman, but the face of a little kid. Cow hormones have the young people all fucked up.

It was still daylight, and I was nervous about being seen. "Oh, I don't know," I said. "I'm just ridin' around." I could smell my sweat, taste the bologna sandwiches I'd had for lunch.

She leaned in the window, looking the car over inside. She wore one of those necklaces strung with candy hearts, and they were melting against her throat. I tried to suck in my gut, but it still rubbed the steering wheel. "I got to be home in two hours," she said.

"Sure," I said. "No problem." For one brief moment, it was like that commercial come true, I swear to God. I was already picturing the stuff we'd do. But then, just as she opened the door to slide in beside me, someone began yelling from across the street. I looked over and saw a tall stocky woman with curlers in her hair standing on the porch of a big red-brick. "Oh, shit," the girl said. "That's my volleyball coach." She stepped away from the car just as the woman leaped off the porch and began running toward us. I blew through two red lights, and then made a fast right out of town. That's the reason I didn't drive the Merc today. I figure every cop in Ross County has a description of Jill's car stuck in his sun visor.

T HIS AFTERNOON WE'VE BEEN OUT TO THE MOTHER-IN-law's for another one of her Sunday dinners—a raw pink chicken stuffed with bits of blue grass that I swear the old bag foraged from an Easter basket—and now my ulcers are screaming for long dogs with sauce and limp, greasy fries. Jill's always on me about my clogged pipes, but I'm a big guy—they don't call me Big Bernie for nothing—and I crave junk food like a baby craves the tit. Besides, I'm beginning to believe that anything I do to extend my life is just going to be outweighed by the agony of living it.

As the row of cars creeps forward, I drift back to one of the daydreams I've been having lately, the farewell one where I douse myself with gasoline, then hand Jill the gold-plated lighter the guys at work gave me when the company forced me into early retirement. "Fire when ready," I say, standing at attention, flipping her a little salute. Fantasizing myself as a brave orange fireball is damn near the only thing that makes me hard anymore; but today, for some reason, I crank it up a notch, and the flames in my mind leap across to Jill's hair, then onto the house, and finally to Jerry. Whoosh! In less time than it takes Larry Fedder to burn a burger, the only thing left of the fucked-up family that lived at 124 Belmont is ashes.

Not that I really would, but I can't help feeling the way I feel, even with the new combo Doc Webb prescribed the other day. I even told him about the commercial, but he dismissed it as postretirement depression. "Just quit watching it," he said.

"How's that?" I asked.

He was standing by the window in his office, staring at the car dealership across the street. "It's like that anthrax scare," he muttered to himself.

"Well, what about the Zippo?" I said. I hauled it out of my pocket and held it up, a final attempt to convince him that I'm a troubled man.

He glanced over his glasses at the shiny lighter, then checked his watch. "Bernard, you shouldn't smoke," he said. Then he handed me a little grab bag of samples and showed me out the door.

I didn't understand what he was trying to say, but I do know my problem has nothing to do with powdered germs or free pills. The poor fuck didn't know what to do, so he was just trying to fluff it up and make the whole ordeal seem like it was happening to somebody else. Everything is too complicated when you're alive, even for the experts.

I PULL UP TO THE SPEAKER AND GO HOG WILD WHILE GRABbing for the sun-bleached antacids I keep on the dash. I order enough junk to tear me up for the rest of the afternoon. The Chevy is missing a little, and my plan is to take it out on the highway and blow the carbon out of it after we put Jerry to bed this evening. "There is a difference," Jill says out of the blue. Though I know better, I ask her what the hell she's talking about. "Between big and fat," she says.

"Big and fat," I repeat slowly, waiting for the goddamn punch line to smack me upside the head.

"Yeah," she says, "I mean, the way I see it, big is like that Arnold guy in the movies, but fat is like your aunt Gloria. So

I've always wondered why they call you Big Bernie and not Fat Bernie."

I tear off three of the crumbly Rolaids and chomp them while staring at the little amplified speaker protruding between the giant photos of the Chocolate Rock and the Dilly Bars. Even if I ate everything on the menu, I'd still be hungry. White foam begins to bubble from my mouth. I look like the rabid dog in the horror movie that Jerry made us play over and over last winter until Jill finally rigged it to look like it broke in the VCR. "Maybe you better sleep in the other room tonight," Jill says, scooting over next to the door.

A station wagon loaded with kids in bathing suits is ahead of us in the line. One little guy in the back keeps messing with us, making gestures with his tongue that kids his age shouldn't know anything about. "Maybe we oughta take him home with us," I joke, making a feeble attempt to turn the lousy day around. I'm kicking myself in the ass now because I bitched so much about the mother-in-law's half-dead chicken. "Many kids as that woman's got, she wouldn't even miss him."

"I think he's eating his own shit," Jill says, and then sticks her big sunglasses on so nobody can see her.

"Oh, Christ, Jill," I say, "what makes you say stuff like that? The kid's just playing around." I make a goofy face at the boy just as he turns around to grab his ice-cream cone. I think back to when Jerry was that age. It makes me feel like shit, thinking it, but there are days when I'd give anything just to be able to prop him out on the curb like a broken appliance for the junk man to haul away. And almost like he can read my mind, Jerry starts making that hacking sound way down in his throat that he's been making all summer. It's the type of noise that makes you grit your teeth.

"Not the kid, you idiot," she says. "Jerry."

Whenever I figure it can't get any worse, it always gets worse. Because I try to follow the rule that we don't talk about Jerry in his presence, I decide not to say anything. Besides, I can't stand the thought of another argument. We've been at it for months. Her latest bitch has been over this old car I'm driving, a souped-up 1959 Chevrolet with big fins that I traded my pickup for so I'd have something to drive to the cruise-ins they put on around here in the fast-food parking lots. It's just an excuse to get out of the house, but Jill's always ragging me, pretending to be jealous of the skanky whores who hang out in the custom vans.

As I pull up to the window, she starts in again about the car shows. "There's no reason you can't take Jerry with you," she says.

I get so sick of explaining it. "Hell," I stutter, "what good's that gonna do you? I mean, even if I was screwing around, Jerry wouldn't know the difference between a piece of ass and your mom's false teeth." I immediately hate myself for saying it, for breaking the rule, for even reacting to the crazy bitch at all. Still, there's no way I'm hauling Jerry to a car show, not even in handcuffs.

I pull the car up and there's the girl that works the window, the one with the twisted chains of baby blond hair and the perfectly calibrated gap between her white teeth. She's like that song about the angel that gives head, and I almost blurt out, *Look, Jill, an angel at the Dairy Queen*, but I catch myself. This girl can have any man who buys a milk shake. She's the type of girl that ends up in one of those damn commercials, tormenting the shit out of every old geezer with cable.

The girl grabs my money in a huff before I can even ask her to sack up the Blizzards. This afternoon she's chewing purple gum, and the way she blows bubbles reminds me of Jill back when we were young and horny, before we lost the map that takes you to places like that. "Hey," I say, turning to Jill, "that girl is the spittin' image of you back when you carhopped at the Sumburger. Remember that?" But it's one of those memories that makes the present only that much more unbearable, and Jill just shakes her head, sinks lower into the seat.

While we wait for the order, I listen to my son try to swallow his tongue and go over the whole fucking mess for the thousandth time. Two years ago, on the night before Jerry was supposed to board the bus for boot camp, he went to a party out in the sticks and never came home. Three days later someone threw him out of a car in front of a hospital in Portsmouth, fifty miles away. We were sitting in the dayroom of the wing where Jerry was transferred after he came out of the coma. The young doctor on duty walked in and stuck a video in the TV. It was that old commercial with an egg frying in a skillet while a voice-over explained that this was your brain on drugs or whatever. I'd seen it a hundred times. They used to play it on the tube back when Jerry was a kid as a warning to stay off the shit. I couldn't believe they still used it. "What about the marines?" I asked. "Shit, he's already AWOL, and he don't even have his uniform yet."

The doctor was crouched down trying to shine a light into Jerry's eyes. He finally shook his head and turned the flashlight off. On the TV, the egg began to pop and sputter in the little pan. The doctor stood up and handed me a card from his coat pocket. "Sorry," he said. "Tell them to call me if they have any questions, but I'm pretty sure they won't want him now." Then he turned and hurried away.

"Look, they've got the same microwave we've got," Jill said that day at the hospital, her voice skipping like one of her old

Wayne Newton records. She was trying to pick pork and beans out of Jerry's hair while he made another attempt to walk through the wall. We'd already planned our golden years—a new camper on Rocky Fork Lake, a hot tub in Jerry's old bedroom. Then three weeks later, poor little Delbert Anderson came to work blowing off about his perfect son, the one that built the telescope for the senior citizens, and I broke his jaw with my lunch bucket. The company had me up front signing my papers before the blood was even dry on the breakroom floor.

The blonde hands me the Coneys, the fries, the melting Blizzards, but she doesn't see me no matter how big and stupid I smile. While I'm still checking the sacks, a jacked-up Camaro full of boys pulls up behind us. They all look like the same model: matching earrings, shaved heads, little goatees sprouted around their mouths like hair around a poodle's ass. They begin honking the horn, and the blonde tells me to move on, that I'm holding up the line. "Sorry," I say, and pull forward without any ketchup.

In the rearview, I see one of the boys say something that makes the girl laugh; then I watch in disbelief as she raises her shirt to show her tits. "Holy shit," I say, stopping the car. "Jerry, damn boy, turn around and check that out." For a moment, the girl's breasts are framed in the window like some advertisement for a new double-scoop sundae. They glow in the blazing sunlight, and I think of soft, precious metal. But even though they're beautiful, it's really her smile that takes my breath away. I'd give anything just to feel the way she feels right now. It's the kind of feeling that people never realize they've had until years later, when it's no longer possible to feel it. "Jerry," I say again, turning around to look at him; but all he does is curl up his lips and make that damn duck sound again.

"Jesus Christ, Bernie, what are you doing?" Jill says.

I don't answer. The boys in the Camaro have noticed me staring at the girl, and one of them starts imitating Jerry, squishing his face up and hanging his head on his chest. The girl is still laughing, but she's pulling her top back down. And though I know that two years ago Jerry would have been right there with them, making fun of the retard, I set the emergency brake and haul my fat ass out of the car. I stand there for a second, pulling my shirt down over my white belly, wondering what I'm supposed to do now; but just before I lose my nerve, one of the boys calls out "Porky," then another squeals, "Oink, oink." Taking a deep breath, I walk back to their car and start kicking the shit out of the side panel. Believe me, I'm just a big tub of lard, but when the driver jumps out, a tall boy with big teeth and barbed wire tattooed around his skinny arms, I knock him down with one punch. I've never hit anyone that hard in my life, not even Delbert Anderson.

Suddenly, the world lights up, as if someone peeled the skin off my eyeballs. I look up at the sky, startled by the giant bloom of blue. But fuck, it's only my sunglasses. I'm so pumped that it takes me a second to realize they've fallen off my face, and when I stoop over to pick them up, the boy tries to bite me. I reach down and grab the front of his shirt. My sweat splatters his shiny head like greasy rain. I pull him up off the pavement and smack him again, busting his lip open. By this time, the others are out of the car yelling shit, but keeping their distance. I realize then that they're afraid of me, and I run at them. I grab the one that was making the stupid faces and bang his head against the hood of the car. A wave of dizziness rushes over me, and I let go of his skinny neck. Teeth marks burn my knuckles. A few drops of blood stain my shirt. I wobble for a second in the heat, then head back to the Chevy and flop down behind the wheel.

Jill's squished up in the corner like she's afraid I'm going to hammer her next, but I just sit there sucking the steamy air through my mouth. Jerry is still making the duck sound, and I finally turn around to look at him. Even after all this time, he's got that angel dust glaze in his eyes, as if torching his brain is the only thing he'll ever remember. His face and neck are broken out in a bumpy red rash from where Jill tried to shave him this morning. His white T-shirt is soaked with slobber, stained with his grandmother's watery gravy. Every time Jerry attempts the duck, his tongue pops out and spit runs off his chin. I fumble around, then pull a napkin from one of the sacks of food and wipe his face. When my hand brushes against his jaw, his eyes close like a puppy's.

The other boys are helping the driver back up. They're talking big now, strutting around like they've got shit in their pants. I stick my head out the window and growl like a dog. Then I give them the finger. The girl in the window yells, "Fat motherfucker!" I turn back around and blast my horn, hold it down for a long minute. "My God," Jill says. "Oh, my God." She's holding her hands over her ears.

"Hey, Jerry," I say, "you wanta drive?" I drop the Chevy into low, and rev the engine until the Dairy Queen's windows are rattling. The customers inside are staring at us and I wave at them. In my side mirror, I see the manager approaching cautiously from behind and talking on a cell phone. Suddenly, gunk breaks loose in the carburetor and a huge puff of black smoke shoots out of the tailpipe.

"You're going to jail," Jill says.

I laugh and pull out fast onto High Street, burning rubber, honking the horn. "Slow down!" Jill screams. "What the hell is wrong with you?"

I slide the Zippo from my pocket and squeeze the small metal case, rub it between my fat, sweaty fingers. It has two dates engraved on it, like a tombstone. I toss the lighter out the window and shift the Chevy into second gear, then stomp the gas pedal and squeal down the street. People hanging out on their porches point at us as we rocket past in third. An old lady grabs a little girl up off the sidewalk. A siren begins to whine in the distance.

Suddenly, happiness rips through me like a sword. Reaching over, I grab Jill's knobby knee, but she shoves my hand away. "Kak, kak!" Jerry squawks, as he bounces forward against his restraints. I dig a hot dog out of the sack and tear the wrapper off, cram it in my mouth. In the rearview, I see a police car coming up fast behind us, all of its lights throbbing. The trees, the signs, the entire world, start to bend backward as we race up the highway. "Kak, kak!" Jerry goes again, and I almost grit my teeth. But then, ramming the gearshift into fourth, I start over.

BLESSED

I WAS ON THE PHONE ONE DAY, TRYING TO UNLOAD A HOT four-wheeler to a deer hunter I knew over in Massieville, when Tex Colburn knocked on my door, introduced himself like he was selling Kirby vacuum cleaners or State Farm. I knew who the fucker was, but I decided to play dumb, just stood there looking at him. He pulled his big hands out of the pockets of his leather jacket, lit a cigarette. "I need a second-story man," he finally said, out of the side of his mouth. I'd heard he talked like that, like he'd watched too many old gangster movies.

"What the fuck's that?" I asked.

"Jesus Christ," he said, shaking his head. "What I got to do, kiss your ass? I need a fuckin' partner."

I glanced over his shoulder, saw his shiny new Mustang parked behind my rusty Pinto. My wife and I had just had a baby, a son named Marshall who constantly needed Pampers and formula and all that other baby shit. We were barely scraping by, and so, though I knew it was always better to work alone, I accepted his offer. Tex Colburn was serious business: front-end loaders, jewelry stores, vintage cars—high-priced stuff that people actually commissioned him to steal. Me, I was pinching push mowers and breaking into mom-and-pop groceries out in the sticks. Hooking up with him was big-time.

I ran with him for over a year and made more money than I'd ever dreamed a thief could make in southern Ohio. My wife and I moved into a fancy apartment, bought a new Monte Carlo, put down a hundred on the Super Lotto every Saturday night. Dee soon lost the baby fat, and I started bringing home a porno two or three nights a week to help rekindle our former fires. For every new position she mastered, I bought her another Longaberger basket. Finally I'd begun to enjoy a certain illegal prosperity.

But then, before my son was old enough to talk, I was nearly killed falling off the roof of Burchwell's Pharmacy in the middle of a rainy night in Meade, Ohio. My first coherent thought after landing on the blacktop with the crowbar still in my hand was that Tex would leave me for the law to find. Then I felt him snatch the tool from my hand, and my second coherent thought was that he was going to finish me off first. That was his way—never leave anything to chance. "Please, Tex," I managed to say, as I lay flat on my back, staring up at the black sky pouring down on me. Waiting for the blow, I suddenly thought about all the hogs I'd knocked in the head with a sledge at the meatpacking plant I'd worked in right after high school. It was the only real job I'd ever had, and I'd held it only six months, but it seemed as if, lying there helpless behind the drugstore, my life was coming full circle. I was going to die the same way I'd slain all those animals.

Instead Tex surprised me with something like compassion,

grabbing me under the arms and dragging me to his Mustang. A few minutes later, we were pulling up outside the big glass doors of the ER at Meade General. Though I could still move my toes, my legs were numb, and every time I took a breath, hot nails of pain shot through my lower back. When he stopped the car, I gasped, "Tex, can you help me inside?"

He snorted and flicked his cigarette out the window at a big potted plant. "Don't push your luck, you shit-for-brains," he said. Then he turned and stared into my eyes until I had to look away. I opened the door. "Don't say anything," he warned.

"I ain't stupid," I said.

"We had a good run," he said. Then, leaning over, he shoved me out onto the concrete and drove away.

An orderly in a white outfit finally came out and led me inside. Though my injuries were severe—a broken collarbone and two crushed disks in my back—the doctor on call that night turned out to be a god. Twelve hours after getting to the hospital, I went home with a bottle of his religion. I never even had to see him again; he'd just phone in the Oxy 'scripts whenever I called and complained. I was cashing in three, sometimes four 'scripts of 80s a month. Because the Oxy was time-released, I learned to lick the coating off the tabs and chop them into powder, then snort them for a quicker delivery. If I was too far gone to handle the razor blade, I'd just chew them up before swallowing. My head became a perfect holiday, my nerves foamy little buds of milk. The Oxy filled holes in me I hadn't even realized were empty. It was, at least for those first few months, a wonderful way to be disabled. I felt blessed.

In reality, though, my life was now on a downward course. Under the influence of the Oxy, I lost even the ambition to steal other people's belongings. Tex picked up a new partner, and the bank repossessed the Monte Carlo. Luckily, we'd kept the Pinto as backup. By the time my opiate honeymoon was over, we were renting a leaky, mildewed trailer on the outskirts of Knockemstiff, the holler where I'd grown up. Though I'd sworn a million times that I'd never go back there, I broke that promise, just like I did all the other vows I'd made before my accident.

The last renters of the trailer had cut a hole in the floor for a toilet after the plumbing went bad. When we moved in, the landlord reluctantly fixed the busted pipes and Dee covered the hole with a piece of plywood that sagged and creaked whenever somebody stepped on it. On a warm day, the stench of strangers' waste hung in the narrow rooms like the thick fog of failure. My son was terrified of falling in the hole because, according to Dee, I'd once threatened him in one of my blackouts that I could stick him down there and he'd never get out. And though I was certain that I must have been joking, it was evident that my sense of humor had been bred out of him.

Every time I came to, it seemed like Dee was lying on the couch in her Marlboro sweatpants, drinking bargain Big K pop from a plastic jug that looked like a gas can, while Marshall scratched the bottoms of her feet with a hairbrush. Sometimes, as I watched her stuff another bag of Fritos into her mouth, I thought about the time I'd invited Tex over for a beer. Walking up to the front door, we could see Dee through the curtains, sitting on the couch with her silk robe parted, letting the baby suck on her swollen brown nipples. She was beautiful that night. "Damn," Tex said. "Would you look at that!"

"Better let me go in first," I said.

Then later, after Dee had gone to bed, as Tex was leaving,

he stopped outside the door and said, "Look, I don't know how you feel about stuff like this, but I'd give a pretty penny for one night with your old lady."

"You're kidding me, right?"

"How 'bout two grand?" he said. Tex was sawed-off and hairy in all the wrong places. "Manly," he called himself, whenever anyone had nerve enough to comment on his fur. He looked like an ape in cowboy boots and a leather jacket.

"I won't ever need your money that bad, Tex," I'd said, shutting the door in his face.

That had been only a couple of years ago. Now Dee was nothing but patches of pimples and rolls of fat. The only thing she seemed capable of doing besides watching the tube was pointing out my defects. And even if she happened to be in a good mood, it was just as horrible. She'd got on this kick where she pretended to be a movie star, and she'd go on for hours about crab cakes and evening gowns and the sunset over some beachfront hideaway. That she stayed with me was just another sign of her indolence. In a more advanced society, they would have probably killed us both and fed our bodies to the dogs.

Meanwhile, Marshall was quickly turning into one of those sullen, creepy kids who never says a word, the kind who goes on to communicate telepathically with a pet rat and sincerely dreams of eternal infamy. It aggravated my condition, all that silence, not even a *Dad Dad*. His muteness was a thorn in my side whenever I was alert. Even retarded talk would have been better than no talk at all. Even a garbled *Fuck you* would have been nice once in a while.

Sometimes I'd suggest to Dee that she have Marshall checked out. "He's deaf!" I'd scream in her ear. "Can't you see he's fucked up!" I'd grab him by his thin shoulders and try to shake a sentence out of him. "Marshall, say something, god-damn it," I'd plead, but when I turned him loose, he'd just roll away in a corner like a ball of lint. Then Dee would act insane and start waving her hands around in some sort of make-believe sign language as if she were making fun of me for caring. If I kept pressing her, she'd warn me that she was on the verge of calling her family over to settle me down. They'd kicked my ass a few times for what they called rude behavior, and I'd become careful about how I performed domestic abuse. So I'd back off and chew another Oxy, then crawl into bed and dismiss Marshall's silence as just another one of those problems that Dee refused to recognize.

Even though I got my medication for free with the welfare card, and the government sent me a check every month for my bad back, we were always broke. Toward the end of the month, we'd run out of all the essentials that make living that sort of life bearable—candy and ice cream and cigarettes—and I'd start hinting to Dee that we should sell some blood. It was the only type of work that I could get her to do. Mine was no good because of my hepatitis, but Dee was AB negative and still pathogen-free, so the technicians welcomed her with open arms. We'd go to Portsmouth and sell a pint at the clinic on Fourth Street, then unload another one at the lab down along the river. By the time they siphoned the second one off, she'd be white as a sheet, as cold as ice. It made her feel special, having that rare blood. It was the only piece of her that anybody still desired.

So one bitterly cold morning in November, we found our-selves driving down the highway on a trip we'd made a hun-dred times, to sell the fluids from her body. The exhaust system on the Pinto was shot, and because carbon monoxide kept spewing up through the rotten holes in the floorboards, we had to roll the windows down to keep from getting gassed. Marshall was sitting in the backseat quiet as a snail and all snotty from a cold, and I shucked off my coat and threw it to him. Yesterday's cereal crud was still caked to his face like dry-wall mud, and the new clothes that Dee had bought him last week were already filthy.

The damp, gray sky covered southern Ohio like the skin of a corpse. The landscape was a seemingly endless row of squat metal buildings full of cheap junk for sale: carpet remnants, used furniture, country crafts. Because Dee had insisted that I do the driving, I'd held off on my morning Oxys, and was feeling a little more on edge than usual. But still, the cold air blowing through the windows was refreshing after a month spent penned up in the trailer. As I drove, I even began to look around for businesses that might be suitable candidates for burglary.

Then Dee started talking her bullshit, stuff about rich celebrities and their private lives. A stranger would have thought she knew these people personally, the way she described their wants and desires. I shut her out, started thinking about the two 80s I'd stashed in the dash for an emergency. "Poor Brad," she said wistfully.

I thought she was commenting on my cousin's bad luck; he'd been arrested again for stealing hubcaps. "Shoot, he'll be out in three months," I said. "That bag biter can do that standing on his head."

"Brad Pitt, you idiot," Dee said.

"Fuck him."

"Oh, believe you me, mister, if I ever got the chance."

"Ha, that's a good one. You hear that, Marshall? Shit, you and a fuckin' donkey maybe."

"Or Tex," she said, sticking her big round face out at me.

"What about Tex, you asshole? Maybe you could even get him ready for me."

"You mention that bastard's name again, I'll knock your teeth out," I said, regretting again that I'd ever told her about the offer of two grand. And though it was true that Tex had driven me to the hospital that night instead of smashing in my head, he'd gone on to ruin my reputation, told around that I'd begged for my life that night behind the drugstore, that I'd offered to suck him off in exchange for mercy. Every day I prayed for his capture.

We were stopped at a red light right outside of Portsmouth when a silver Lexus pulled up beside us. Glancing over, I was startled by the bold, sparkling eyes of the most stunning woman I'd ever seen. She was checking us out, laughing into her cell phone. Every inch of her radiated money and happiness and fine genes. Though there had once been a time when I would have yelled over and asked her to fuck, now all I felt was shame that she'd had to look at me at all. My hair was uncombed and greasy, my teeth coated with yellow scum, my tattoos meaningless and outdated. I turned my head and waited for the light to change.

As the Lexus sped on down the street, I let out the slippery clutch on the Pinto and started cramping. Because of the opiates, I seldom ate anything but candy bars and ice cream, but that morning Dee had insisted on stopping at Mickey D's for breakfast. I'd poisoned myself with sausage gravy and biscuits and Egg McMuffins and a chocolate shake. By the time we got downtown, I knew I couldn't hold it. "Jesus Christ, stop somewhere," Dee said. But I couldn't face the public now. All I could see was that beautiful woman in the fancy car turning her nose up at me.

Though I fought it, tensing my muscles and squeezing the

steering wheel with both hands, the pains kept getting worse. Desperate, I turned down an alley and saw a Dumpster behind an old brick building. I stomped the parking brake and jumped out. Diving behind the metal container, I jerked my pants down and cut loose. For a second, the relief was better than any drug, but then I heard tires crunching in the gravel behind me. Looking around, I saw a police car approaching slowly. I was trapped, my skinny ass shining at the two officers inside. There was no way I could stop—the stuff was pouring out of me like pancake batter. I gave a little wave, cursing them under my breath.

As the two cops got out of the cruiser, I tried to stand, but another wave of cramps forced me down into a squat again. I saw shit splatter on my jeans, inside and out. "What the hell we got here, Larry?" one of the cops said, an older man with a red nose and a thick mustache. He pulled a black club out of a holster attached to his belt.

Foul watery slime squirted from me again, and I lowered my head. "I ain't sure, Dave," the other cop said, a young man with sharp features, muscles sticking out of his shirtsleeves. "The only thing that I ever see doing that in public is a dog." He kicked some loose gravel at me. "Are you a dog, you dirty bastard?" he asked me.

"No," I managed to say.

"Check him out, Larry," the older cop said with a chuckle. "I'll cover you."

"Fuck, I ain't touching that skanky bastard," the younger cop said. "He's probably got the AIDS or something."

They stood there for a minute watching me, then the older cop said, "Dog, where in the hell do you think you are?"

"Portsmouth," I said.

"Stand up when he's talking to you," the younger cop ordered.

"I can't," I groaned. "I'm still sick."

Then he pointed his gun at me. "I said to stand up, motherfucker."

I stood up, holding my pants out of the mess with my hands. "Put your hands in the air," the older cop said. I bit my lip, then raised my hands and let my jeans drop to the ground.

"Now, I want you to march in place, like you're in my army," the younger cop said, nudging his partner with his elbow. "You know how to do that, dog?" They both stepped back. I raised one knee, then lowered it and pressed my jeans down into the spreading puddle. As I lifted the other leg, I looked over and saw Dee scoot behind the wheel, a blank look on her face. Marshall had covered his head with my coat. If I could have wrestled a gun from one of the cops, I gladly would have killed us all at that moment.

"Please, officers," I said, my voice shaking. "I don't want no trouble. I got my family in the car."

The older cop looked over at the Pinto. "Go call in the plate," he told his partner. Then, as the younger cop walked back to the cruiser, he asked me, "Where you from, dog?"

"Meade," I answered. "Can I pull my pants back up now?"

"Not yet," he said.

We stood in the cold until the other cop came back and said the car was clean. "All right, go the fuck back where you come from," the older cop said.

"Yeah, and you better think twice before you take a shit in Portsmouth again," said the muscled one. Then they both busted a gut as they walked to the cruiser.

I pulled my pants up and watched them back down the alley, then I started to get in the car. "You're not getting in here like that," Dee said. I looked around, pulled a flattened cardboard box out of the Dumpster and laid it on the passenger seat. "Oh, God," she said when I slid in and slammed the door shut. "You should kill yourself." My jeans and hands were pasted with shit.

Jerking open the glove box, I fumbled around for the Oxy I'd brought with me. "It'll be all right," I said as I chewed the tablets up, and tried to calm down.

"Oh, Marshall, did you hear that?" Dee said sarcastically. "Daddy says everything is going to be just fine and fuckin' dandy." She wheeled out of the alley and drove a block down the street, then pulled over. Even with the windows open, the smell of me was sickening. "Walk over there and clean up," Dee said, pointing to a Chinese restaurant across the street.

"Just go sell the fuckin' blood," I said. "I ain't going nowhere. It's your goddamn fault I got sick in the first place."

Twisting around in the seat, she began punching at me wildly. "I should make you get out right here, you sonofabitch," Dee screamed.

"Fuck you," I said, grabbing her fists. "And keep your voice down before those fuckin' cops come back."

"We're going home," she said, breaking loose of my grip and jamming the car into gear.

"I'll be goddamned. Go to the clinic."

"It's my blood, you bastard."

"Jesus Christ, Dee," I said. "Please."

"No. Things got to change."

She headed the car north on High; we were going home empty-handed after all that trouble. I lit my last cigarette and stared out the window. By the time we reached Waverly, the pills I'd swallowed had cast me into a sweet, warm ocean. For the next few minutes, I dreamily considered changing my life; I decided to quit the Oxy once I'd finished the 'script I was on. With the right therapy, I could land a decent job. I saw myself as a construction foreman, maybe even a drug counselor. We'd move out of the stinking trailer and into a nice house. I could see us in church on Sundays, our son singing in the choir. And then I nodded off.

When I woke up, I was lost and confused. Darkness had settled all around me, and I was shivering with the cold. It took me a minute or two to figure out that I was sitting in the Pinto in front of our trailer. As I started to climb out, I discovered the cardboard box stuck to my backside. For a few seconds, I thought that some sonofabitch had pulled a sick joke on me, but then I recalled the trip to Portsmouth, the cops in the alley, the fight with Dee. I dropped back down into the seat, lit my lighter and searched around for another pill. But the dash was empty. Then, getting out of the car, I tore the cardboard off me and got more of the cold, clammy shit on my hands.

Stumbling up to the concrete porch and digging for my house key, I happened to glance in the window. Dee and Marshall were cuddled together on the couch like two happy birds. They were eating toast and crumbs were flying everywhere, my son was talking so fast. I watched his lips moving, forming words I'd never heard him say. I pressed my ear to the door, my heart pounding, and listened to his excited, stuttering voice. For a moment, I thought I was witnessing some kind of miracle. But then, as I stood there, I slowly began to realize that Marshall had been talking all along, just not around me.

I stepped away from the door and took a deep breath of the cold air. I realized I was in the middle of one of those moments in life where great things are possible, if a person is willing to make the right choice. A car drove by, shining its headlights on me, and suddenly I knew what I had to do. I could already see myself coming back in a year or two, clean and ready to do right by my family. Everyone would praise me, maybe even forget my past. But then I thought about the bottle of Oxy in the medicine cabinet and I stopped. I lifted my filthy hands and smeared the shit across my face, through my hair. Turning back, I grabbed hold of the door handle, and stuck my key in the lock. I heard everything go silent and sad inside the trailer as I pushed the door open, but I didn't care. Just one more time, just once more before I left, I needed to feel blessed.

HONOLULU

HALF THE TIME NOW THE ONLY THING CRAWLING AROUND in Howard Bowman's worn-out head is that four-letter word, the one swear that his wife no longer allows in the house. Back when he was still in good shape, Peg gave him an ultimatum. "No more, Howard. If you say that damn word one more time, I'm leaving. My Lord, you got the grandkids saying it." Now look at him, afraid to say it, the only goddamn thing that makes sense anymore. Fuck. Fuck. Fuck.

SITTING STRAIGHT UP IN HIS STICKY PLASTIC RECLINER, Howard peers into the large photograph hanging on the wall while methodically twisting curly gray hairs out of his left arm. Peg's always pestering him with a new goal—names, dates, numbers—but every morning it's as if another fuse has popped, another important connection ripped out of his brain while he was sleeping. Sometimes he wishes the woman would just let him rot. He yearns for the day when he'll be wiped clean.

Earlier today, she flew into the living room and said, "Okay, Boss, see that picture?" Howard jerked awake, looked up at her with a pained expression. "On the wall over there," Peg pointed. "Your retirement picture? Give me the names of those men by suppertime," she told him, bending over and scraping a dab of oatmeal off his chin with the corner of her apron.

Howard stared blankly at the wall. Something was expected of him. "Which one?" he finally asked, just as he lifted his thin leg and squeaked out a small pocket of gas.

Peg groaned and took a step back. "All of them, Howard. You worked with those people at the paper mill. Remember?"

"Y-e-s," he said slowly, lightly stroking the hair on his left arm like some kind of pet.

"Good," she said. "Here, better write them down." She handed Howard a little notebook and pen, then walked over and turned the TV off. "What about the bathroom?" she asked. "Do you need to go?"

Howard looked around the room, under the coffee table. The tall, big-boned woman was standing in the doorway, still watching him. "There's a lot of them," he said.

H E STUDIES THE PHOTOGRAPH ALL AFTERNOON, HIS EYES slowly turning to sand, but the only thing he can recall is that the little guy wearing the railroad hat used to buy a new Lincoln every year. Hell, even the supervisors couldn't afford that. Out in the kitchen, Peg drops a pan that bounces across the cold linoleum, sounds like a goddamn cymbal clanging in his ears. Lately every little noise gets on his nerves, tears his guts up, makes him forget shit that no man should ever forget.

Glancing out the big picture window, Howard watches the new neighbors fall out of their trailer laughing, roll around in the snow like dogs. Convinced the ponytailed man and his fat wife were thieves from the moment they moved in across the road, Howard had Peg buy locked gas caps for both vehicles, but so far all he's seen the bastards do is hang a dead ground-hog from the maple tree. "We'll be damn lucky if the sheriff even finds our bodies," Howard predicted, when he first saw the swollen carcass rocking in the breeze like a kid's swing. He watches them jump into a banged-up Festiva plastered with bumper stickers advertising OHIO'S SCENIC CAVERNS and some-thing called MONSTER MAGNET, then burn a little patch of rub-ber in front of Howard's mailbox. A trail of black smoke follows them all the way up the road. A valve job, Howard thinks, and starts to write a note to himself to check the oil in the Buick. But then, in that mysterious way his memory works now, he suddenly recalls a night in Honolulu and a shipmate's name. He yells for Peg.

"What?" she asks, sticking her head through the doorway.

"That guy I was telling you about the other day—the one from New York—his name was . . . Damn, I had it. Had a nose like a . . . that guy's nose was . . ."

"Jesus, Howard, what about the people on the wall?" Peg yells. "You know what the doctor said. If you don't try, it's only going to get worse." Suddenly, she stops and leans against the wall, takes a deep breath, counts to ten silently. "Okay, how many did you get?" she asks, her voice careful and quiet now.

"His nose was like a . . ." he replies.

She walks over and takes the notepad from his hand. "Oil," she reads aloud. "That's it? Oil? Oil what?"

Howard throws the pen across the room, then picks up the remote and stabs at the buttons until the TV pops on. A rodeo coming from Atlantic City prances across the screen. Tilting the recliner back with a hard thump, he stares red-faced at a sequined girl standing in the middle of the ring doing rope tricks.

"All right then, take a break," Peg says, looking down at her husband. "We'll eat maybe in an hour." She wants to ask him if he's been to the bathroom, but he's already upset. Turning, she goes back into the kitchen. Howard's made her promise that no one will ever pin a diaper on him, as if she'll actually have a choice in the matter.

It is true that he keeps forgetting his life, but a few minutes later Howard suddenly remembers the time he and that crazy bastard from New York picked up the white floozy on that street corner in Honolulu where the little crippled Samoan sold flowers. She wore a red dress, carried a straw purse with a broken wooden handle, kept licking a cold sore on her upper lip that was as big as one of those tropical roaches. The way she walked ahead of them shaking her big ass reminded Howard of the story about the flute guy that drowned all those rats in the river; but the woman led them instead to a pink motel that advertised a radio in every room, which was pretty plush for Honolulu in 1952. Howard was up for anything that night, but when the woman turned on the light, he saw the little baby asleep in a shoe box in the corner. It reminded him of the Baby Jesus picture that Maude Speakman had tacked up in the store back home. "Hey, there's a kid here," Howard said, as if someone had forgotten it when they checked out.

"Yeah," the whore said, undoing the big black buttons on her wrinkled dress. "I named him Cary, like that new movie star."

"What? You mean he's gonna watch us?" Howard asked.

"What's the big deal?" the woman said. "He's asleep. Besides, he ain't but three months. He don't know nothing."

"Don't pay no attention to him, honey," the guy from New

York said. "Howie's from some dump in Ohio they call Knockemstiff. Shit, he ain't never even had a pizza."

"Lady, there ain't no way," Howard said angrily. "Lord, you oughta be put in jail."

Damn, Howard thinks, suddenly leaning forward in the squeaky chair. I almost had it, that bastard's name. Always laughing, that fucking guy. Had a nose like a tomato . . . like a banana . . . like a . . .

But ol' New York had already dropped his pants, already said, "Look, babe, we ain't here for no kissy-face. Just bend over and say your prayers." Before he realized what he was doing, Howard grabbed the baby and ran out the door. He can still see New York's hairy hands reaching around to squeeze the whore's big tits and the two pale streams of milk shooting out all over the thin plaid bedspread. Howard lugged the tiny baby down the hot street, sat on a bench under a brown palm tree crawling with bugs the size of gumballs, counted each car that passed by until he figured New York had shot his three dollars' worth.

P EG RUSHES INTO THE LIVING ROOM, GRABS HER PURSE OFF the piano. "We're clear out of Crisco. You need anything?"

"Like what?" Howard asks suspiciously.

"I won't be long," she assures him, fluffing her flat gray hair in the mirror. "What's my birthday, Howard?" Peg asks suddenly.

"What? Who?"

"My birthday. Try to have it when I get back, okay?" She pats him on the shoulder.

"Are you leaving?" he says.

He watches the woman back out the driveway in his wife's

car and wonders what ever happened to the people he used to know. Jesus Christ, even that kid in the motel would be damn near fifty now.

The TV rodeo drags on, high-strung horses and killer bulls and clowns that fart and shoot blue flames across the corral. Howard's sure they're trying to do him in with all the grease, all that goddamn noise every day, but then he seems to recall that they went somewhere far away.

I mean, I served four years with that guy, Howard thinks, fighting to hold on to the memory. I was in the United States Navy. The whore had a blond wig pinned to her head that tilted all over the place like the one that stupid clown's wearing on the TV.

When he returned to the motel with the baby, the New York prick razzed Howard about stuff right in front of the woman, said she was tight as a mouse's ear. Howard's face turned purple, and the woman laughed, asked if he was ready to get his cherry popped. He dropped the baby on the bed like he was trying to bounce a basketball, got the hell out of there. Poor little guy never made a sound.

He was a good kid, Howard thinks to himself, but somehow that's just not good enough.

Jumping up, he quickly walks down the hallway to the spare bedroom. He's got detailed instructions written out like a recipe hidden in his wallet, but he doesn't need them today. Reaching under the dresser, he pulls out a rolled-up piece of plastic, then spreads it on the floor. He stands there lost for a moment, then removes his dentures, wipes them on his pants, sticks them in the front pocket of his shirt. Howard still remembers where he stashed the pistol in the bottom drawer, which, just for a second, almost convinces him to wait another day. But then, easing himself down on the floor, his dried-out joints cracking like old pine, he pulls one end of the plastic up over his head like a hood, sets the barrel against his soft palate. He clicks the safety off. He smells his bad breath, wonders if he'll shit his pants. "Okay," he says to himself, "just squeeze the goddamn thing." For the first time in ages, there's nothing left to remember.

But then there's a noise, somebody coming through the back door, probably that damn woman again, or maybe those fucking robbers from across the road. Howard lies there on the floor with the gun barrel cutting his gums and listens. He should do something, but then he'd have to start all over again. They've got balls to break into a man's home, no doubt about that. Sure as hell they're going to siphon the gas out of his truck. Christ, he thinks, the sons of bitches must be looking for the key.

He tastes blood and suddenly remembers the time his dad caught Bill Willard stealing gas out of his old Ford tractor, right after Howard went off to boot camp up at the Great Lakes. Damn, it was cold up there. The old man later wrote Howard that he'd told everyone in Hap's Bar that Bill could suck a hose better than any damn woman in Knockemstiff, maybe the whole state of Ohio. Scrawled HA! HA! in big black letters that took up half the page. It was the only letter his father sent him all the time he was in the service; shit, probably the only letter Floyd Bowman wrote in his entire life. Staring up at the ceiling, Howard watches the shadows of early evening float across the wavy old plaster like the ghosts that swim in his head.

OUT IN THE KITCHEN, PEG'S BUSY, COOKING WITH ONE hand, gripping the phone in the other. She dumps sliced potatoes into the hot skillet, along with some chopped onion, and then steps back from the sputtering grease. "He must be asleep," she says quietly into the phone. "They gave him some new stuff that just knocks him for a loop." She covers the skillet with a lid and adjusts the flame, then bends down to light a cigarette from the stove. "No way," Peg says. "Believe me, it's easier just to cook at home. He started up with that F word the last time we were in Bob Evans and just wouldn't stop. Lord, I wanted to crawl under the table."

Sitting down at the kitchen counter, she takes a long weary drag on her cigarette as she listens to her daughter on the other end of the line go on about stuff she knows nothing about yet. "Carrie, you don't understand," Peg finally says, stubbing her cigarette out. "Your daddy's second-stage already. He don't even know me half the time." Standing up, she tries to smooth the wrinkles out of her long corduroy dress. "No, all he talks about is Hawaii," Peg sighs, looking out the window as the evening sun dives like a flaming bird into that other world. And just like that, for one brief beautiful moment, as the crashing rays turn the kitchen a bright blood-red, she forgets everything.

THE FIGHTS

JIM PEERED AT ME OVER HIS WHITE CUP. "HOW'S THAT OLD man of yours doing?" he asked. We were shooting the shit in the Bridge Street Diner. I was smoking his cigarettes and drinking their coffee. Jim was my AA sponsor, and we'd just been to the Friday Night Sober N' Crazy Group over at the Lutheran church on High Street. He liked to stop by the diner after the meeting and check for new piercings on the bony blonde who worked the late shift. He was old, but he still liked to look at the young stuff. Every time the little wench bent over a table, he whimpered like a dog having a bad dream.

"He's hanging in there as far as I know." I shrugged, blew on my coffee. Though I seldom mentioned my father to anyone, I'd told Jim a couple of weeks ago that the old man's heart had taken a turn for the worse. According to my sister, the surgeons said there wasn't any more they could do. Jeanette was always calling and giving me updates on the situation. She worried enough for the whole family, and then some. "Too much scar tissue," she'd tell me every time. *He's not the only one*, I felt like saying.

Jim nodded, took another drag from his Kool. "What about that money you stole?" he said. "You take care of that yet?"

Jesus Christ, I thought, I never should have told him. "It was only twenty fucking dollars," I said. "You make it sound like I took their life savings." The last time I'd visited my parents, I'd slipped a lousy Andy Jackson out of my mother's purse. Though I wasn't drinking anymore, I was still messed up in a lot of ways.

"I don't care if it was a fucking nickel. It's still important, goddamn it," Jim said. "You can't start being honest, you'll never stay off the sauce." He made such a big deal out of telling the truth that I figured he was constantly fighting the urge to spin a tremendous whopper.

I nodded my head. I didn't want to argue. Jim was a black man, and anytime I was around him, I had to be careful with my language. Though I was getting better, I was still afraid of letting a *nigger* or a *coon* slip out of my mouth whenever he pissed me off. Old habits are hard to break. In the holler where I'd grown up, everyone was white. The only time we ever saw black people was when we went into Meade to buy groceries or pay the electric bill. There were hillbillies in Knockemstiff, Ohio, who wouldn't watch a TV show that had blacks in it. My old man was one of the worst.

Jim rubbed his chin, twisted a kink out of his old wrinkled neck. "You do want to stay sober, don't you, Bobby?" His gray hair was as thick and wiry as a Brillo pad, and his skin shone like wet black tar under the fluorescent lighting. Whenever he spoke at lead meetings, he told stories about trolling the bars near the paper mill for free drinks, red-eyed and stinking of piss, pretending to be deaf and dumb. He'd let white guys try to knock his teeth out for a pint of Thunderbird. Now he drove a jade-colored Cadillac, owned a landscaping outfit with three crews. He was all business when it came to Alcoholics Anonymous, an old-time Big Book thumper who could sometimes be a royal pain in the ass, but it had kept him sober fifteen years.

I glanced over at him, thought about the last couple of years that I drank. A lot of people get the wrong impression, think there's something romantic or tragic about hitting bottom. Every so often, strange men knocked on my door and threatened to kick my ass for something they said I had done. Sometimes I hid in the corner of the room, afraid to even breathe, and other times I called their bluff. Once a detective had me picked up for a rape, and I had to admit in the interrogation room that I couldn't remember one way or another. Thank God he later determined that I wasn't the type of pervert they were looking for. I went bankrupt, and caught the crabs, and broke my nose on a sidewalk. I stalked my ex-wife and missed so much work at the paper mill that even the union got sick of fighting for me. A few months after I lost my job, I woke up in a charity rehab wrapped in an army blanket. My roommate was an old puker seething with yellow sores. His name was Hobo, and he'd once had a glass eye but had lost it somewhere along the way. I grew afraid, started going to meetings.

"Jim, I wouldn't be sitting here in this goddamn place if I didn't," I said. I started to reach for his cigarettes, but he placed his hand over the pack.

"Then you go and have a nice visit with your folks this weekend," he said. "And while you're there, you pay that money back to your poor old mother."

"Yeah, okay," I said. "I hear you."

"Do you need a loan?"

"No," I said. "I just got paid."

"Good." Two streams of smoke drifted from his nostrils as he stubbed out his cigarette and shook another from his pack. He handed it to me. Then he slid out of the booth and dug in his pocket for some change to sprinkle on the table. "We all fuck up, Bobby. Just got to keep trying, that's all." Slapping me on the shoulder, he took one more look at the blonde and left me with the check.

The next day I put on the shirt that I'd bought with the money I'd stolen from my mother and drove out to Knockemstiff. Though I never wanted to live there ever again, it still saddened me to see how much the place had changed in the last few years. Both the store and the bar were closed now, and new houses covered with vinyl were crammed together in the fields that had once been filled with corn and hay. My younger brother's rusty pickup was sitting in the driveway, the back glass covered with NASCAR stickers and a Confederate flag. A weathered squirrel's tail hung from the radio antenna. As I walked up to the front porch, I could see my old man through the big picture window in the living room. The twin stems of an oxygen tube were stuck up his nose, and he was all laid back in his blue luxury recliner, the chair my sister had bought him after his heart blew the first rod. He'd had at least three heart attacks since then, each worse than the one before.

He was watching the fights with my brother. I didn't even have to go inside to figure that out. After he got sick, the only thing my old man enjoyed in life was watching men beat the shit out of each other. The worse somebody got hurt, the better he liked it. Most of the fights took place in seedy Indian casinos between men who were just like him, though he'd never admit it. He had my sister record every minute of boxing that came down from her satellite, and then he watched the tapes all day long as if he were studying for some kind of comeback.

I went in through the breezeway. I found my mother at the kitchen table, her papery hands wrapped around a cup of milky coffee. She was watching another TV. "Hi, stranger," she said, struggling to pull her attention away from the movie that had her hypnotized. "Ooh, I like that shirt. Where'd you get it?"

"Penney's." I bent over and kissed her on top of the head, then poured a cup of coffee from the pot on the counter. Sitting next to the powdered creamer was the purse I'd ransacked during my last visit. Turning back to her, I winked and walked down the short hallway leading to the living room.

"I'll be damned," my old man said. "Look who's here." My father used to be the roughest sonofabitch in the holler, but now his skin was gray and the flesh on his arms hung as loose as an old woman's. He had barely made it through the sixth grade, grew up in a family that traded his labor for sacks of flour and plugs of tobacco. He'd pounded spikes on the railroad at fifteen, been a boxer in the army. I'd once seen him damn near kill a man with his fists at the Torch Drive-in. All my life, I'd carried around the knowledge that I could never be that tough. But there was little of that man left now.

"What's going on?" I said, sitting down on the edge of a chair. My brother, Sam, was lying on the couch, his long ponytail hanging over the end cushion, the brown tip of it nearly touching the wooden floor. He was a stringy but strong man, like my father had been before he got sick, rode a Harley even in the winter, shoed horses for beer money. Sam still lived in my parents' basement when he wasn't shacked up with some

welfare puss, and though he'd never been convicted of anything major, he looked like he'd spent his entire life in prison.
My old man had always played favorites, and most of the love
he had inside him had been spent on my little brother.

"That nigger's takin' a helluva beating, that's what's going
on," Sam said, a hint of glee in his voice.

"Aw, the black bastard," my old man said. I looked at the
TV. Two men, one black, one Hispanic, stood in the middle of
the ring holding on to each other for dear life.

"Who's fighting?" I said. I took a sip of coffee, wished we
were still allowed to smoke in the house.

"Two nobodies," the old man said. "They shouldn't even
be in there."

Sam rose up off the couch and jabbed the air with his
fists. "Goddamn it," he yelled at the TV, "kiss him, why don't
cha?"

I sighed and glanced around the room at the family photos
on the walls. One showed our sweaty family standing at the
edge of the Grand Canyon in 1970. My brother is still in diapers. A toothless Indian had snapped the photo with our camera for a dollar. It was supposed to be our summer of national
monuments, but turned out to be just another fucked-up
episode in our lives. As we'd approached the rim that afternoon, the old man had blackened my mother's eye for trying to
defend me. She was always taking punches for somebody else
back in those days. I was twelve years old, and I'd puked up a
fried egg sandwich that the old man had forced me to eat at a
truck stop. He swore that I was going to eat chicken parts all
the way back to Ohio. In the photograph, he is the only one
smiling. His lean muscles fill out his tight T-shirt, and his eyes
are squinted against the bright Arizona sun. He looks like he is
having a good time.

"What's that on your lip?" the old man said. He was star-ing at my thin mustache, another one of my sorry attempts to reinvent myself.

"Nothing," I said, turning away from the picture.

He looked back over at the fight, adjusted the red-and-yellow comforter that covered him. "I had a full beard when I was fourteen year old," he said.

"What kind of money you makin' at that pizza outfit?" Sam asked.

"It pays the bills," I said. I didn't want to talk about it. Jim had insisted I get a job after rehab, and slinging pies at Tommy's Pizza was the best I'd been able to do so far. Whenever business slowed down, I had to stand out along the main drag with a nervous retard named Joey holding a plastic banner that adver-tised the latest $3.99 special. Every time some bastard blew their horn or gave us the bird, Joey spun around like a Frisbee and dropped his end of the sign. We spent half of our time picking it back up off the ground. I kept hoping he'd get canned or sent back to the handicap school for more training.

"You still on the wagon?" the old man asked.

"Five months now."

"Damn," he said, "that's a long time without a cold one." After my brother was born, the old man had quit drinking the hard stuff on his own, but he still liked his beer. He reached down and adjusted a valve on top of the oxygen tank. "What about those alcohol meetings? You still got to go?"

"I hit one about every day."

"Do you ever see a guy there named Jim Woodfork? Someone told me he goes there."

I thought about it for a second. I wasn't supposed to tell who I saw at meetings. Jim was pretty strict about that. "Well," I started to say, "I ain't—"

"That crazy sonofabitch," my old man said, shaking his head. "He'd do damn near anything for a drink. He was the worst I ever saw."

"Yeah, I know him," I said.

"He wouldn't remember it now he was so drunk, but one time he let me damn near beat him to a pulp for a dollar. Just so he could buy another fifth of goddamn wine. That was probably the best dollar I ever spent in my life."

"He does pretty good now," I said.

"That's what I hear," he said. Then he shrugged. "He's still a nigger though, ain't he, Bobby?"

I looked up from my empty cup. He was grinning at me, a mean look in his pale blue eyes, waiting for an answer. I wondered if somehow he knew that Jim was my sponsor. "Yeah," I finally said, looking away, "he's still a nigger." Then I stood up and walked back out to the kitchen.

My mom shook her head. "I think he's getting worse," she whispered. She was always making this pronouncement about the old man, as if at one time he'd actually been better.

"Agnes, what the hell are you talking about?" the old man yelled from his chair. He had ears like a dog. When we were growing up, he used to beat us kids for whispering behind his back. "Teaching 'em how to dance," he called it. And though those days were over now, though he couldn't even take a piss without dragging along a tank of air, we were all still afraid of him, even my badass brother.

My mother grabbed her TV remote and lowered the volume. "I was just telling Bobby about Jeanette's promotion." She looked at me and shrugged. Mom had told me months ago that Jeanette had finally made assistant manager at the discount store where she'd worked for years.

"Promotion, shit," the old man hollered, his voice suddenly

hoarse and weak. "Did I tell you that goddamn Clyde Chaney's daughter got her nursin' license? Clyde says she's making thirty-two dollars an hour. By God, I'd call that a job, wouldn't you, Bobby?"

I thought about the six bucks an hour I was making at Tommy's Pizza, and I tried not to think about all the shit the old man was saying about me when I wasn't around. "Yeah," I yelled back at him.

"That's it," I heard him say, "kill the black bastard."

For a few minutes, my mom and I sat at the kitchen table in silence. She watched the TV but never bothered to turn the sound back up, and I stared out the window at the field behind the house. It was a damp March evening and a soft gray mist was easing down from the woods on the other side of the creek. A deer loped across the pasture and jumped effortlessly over a sagging fence. In the living room, a bell ended another round.

"So," I finally said to my mom, "what movie you watching?"

"Oh, I don't know the name of it," she said. "I haven't been paying that much attention. It's a murder movie, I think." She slipped a cookie from a pack on the table and dipped it in her coffee.

Just then my brother strolled into the kitchen. Pulling up his T-shirt, he made a big show of rubbing his hairy belly. A faded tattoo of a yellow Tweety Bird peeked through the brown fur. He grabbed a bowl from the cabinet above the sink and dipped some chili from a pot on the stove. "I got some brewskies out in the truck you get thirsty," he said to me.

"And I got you a job delivering pizzas if you ever decide you want to go to work," I replied.

He pointed his spoon at me and squished his face up like

he was on the verge of busting into tears. Then he laughed and started back toward the living room, blowing on the chili as he went. I heard the old man say, "Watch it, honey. That looks hot."

"Jesus, I don't see how you stand it," I said to my mother in a low voice. I walked outside and lit a cigarette. It was nearly dark by then, and I wandered deep into the front yard before I remembered the money I was supposed to pay back to my mother. Next time, I told myself. Wood smoke from a neighbor's house hung in the chilly air. I thought about all those years as a kid when we'd been forbidden to step over the fences my father had erected around his property. He had always been in control of everything that touched his life, but now he couldn't even manage his own heart. Somewhere over the next hill, a dog barked three or four times, and up the road a car engine sputtered and died. I'd grown up here, but it had never felt like home.

I turned and looked at the old man through the window. He was still watching the men on TV beat each other senseless for a chance at happiness. With my father everything had always been about the fight, and I sadly realized that we would never really know each other before he passed. For the first time since I'd been sober, I began to crave a drink. Even the smell of the wood smoke reminded me of whiskey. As I stood there, I recalled something that Jim told me every time he saw me. "You pick up the phone and call me before you take that first one, Bobby. At least give me that much respect." But I'd called him a nigger behind his back, just to please my bitter old man, and I wasn't sure I could ask for anybody's help tonight.

My father suddenly punched the air and whooped loud enough that I could hear him outside. The look on his face was ecstatic. Then the plastic tube slipped from his nose, and I watched him grab for it. For a moment he seemed to hesitate, as if he might be considering his other option, and it became clear to me that he was tired of it all. But after glancing over at my brother, he carefully fastened the hose back in place. He took a deep breath, and I took one with him. The TV light brightened and then dimmed. Tossing my cigarette in the grass, I turned and started toward my car. The fight was nearly over.

ACKNOWLEDGMENTS

First, I'd like to say that, though the stories in this book were inspired by a real place, Knockemstiff, Ohio, all of the characters are fictional. I grew up in the holler, and my family and our neighbors were good people who never hesitated to help someone in a time of need.

Since this is my first book, I have a lot of people to thank: first and foremost, Michelle Herman, writer, teacher, and mentor, who believed in me when I needed it most; Michael Kardos, who pulled "Bactine" from the slush pile and didn't send it back; Kyle Minor, my chief adviser in all things literary; my professors, past and present, all of whom have taught me so many things: Erin McGraw, Lee K. Abbott, Kathy Fagan, and Lee Martin at Ohio State University, and Ron Salamone and Veena Kasbekar at Ohio University.

Another round of thanks go to all of my peers in the workshops at Ohio State University, including Jesse Quillian, Doug Watson, Bart Skarzynski, Laurel Gilbert, Maureen Traverse, Kim Brauer, Loranne Temple, Libby Lantz, Brian Wade, and

Joe Oestreich; oh, yeah, and that poet guy, Pablo Tanguay; Valerie Vogrin at *Sou'wester*; Kelly Daniels and the rest of the gang at *Third Coast*; and Richard Burgin at *Boulevard*.

Also, I'd like to say howdy to all my old friends and co-workers at the paper mill in Chillicothe, Ohio; and offer up a big, big thank-you with all my heart to my parents, Donald and Violet Pollock; my daughter, Amber; and my two grand-daughters, Madison and Rachel.

A very special thanks goes to the great Richard Pine, the equally fantastic Nathaniel Jacks, and the wonderful Susan Hobson at InkWell Management. And last, but certainly not least, I want to thank Gerry Howard, my kickass editor, and everyone else at Doubleday who helped make this book a reality.